THE
CHASE OF THE RUBY

BY

RICHARD MARSH

British Library Cataloguing-in-Publication Data
A catalogue record for this book is available from the
British Library

Contents

Richard Marsh

Richard Bernard Heldmann – better-known by his pseudonym, Richard Marsh – was born in England in 1857. He was educated at Eton and Oxford University, and began to publish short stories shortly after graduating. He published his first novel, *The Mahatma's Pupil*, in 1893, and went on to produce almost twenty more. By far Marsh's greatest commercial success came with his early work *The Beetle* (1897). A story about a mysterious oriental figure who pursues a British politician to London, and wreaks havoc using his powers of hypnosis and shape-shifting, the novel is in a similar vein to other sensational turn-of-the-century fictions such as George du Maurier's *Trilby* (1894) and Bram Stoker's *Dracula* (1897). Marsh also produced a good body of short fiction. He died in 1915, aged 57.

CHAPTER I.
GHOSTS IN AFRICA

'Upon my word, this is—' He hesitated, then chose another form of words with which to conclude his sentence. 'This is extraordinary.'

He allowed the paper to flutter from between his fingers, stood staring at nothing, then, stooping, picked up the sheet of blue post from where it had fallen at his feet.

'Extraordinary!' he repeated.

He regarded it and handled it as if it had been some uncanny thing—though, on the face of it, it was nothing of the kind. It was a formal letter addressed to 'Guy Holland, Esq., 37A Craven Street, W.C.' It began 'Dear Sir,' and ended 'Yr. obedt. servant, SAML. COLLYER.' Between the beginning and the end it informed him that his uncle, George Burton, had died at Nice on February 23, and that the writer would feel obliged if he would call upon him at his earliest possible convenience.

'I wonder if I saw him die?' Mr Holland knit his brows as he asked himself the question. 'How could I, when I was in Mashonaland and he was in Nice? Absurd!'

He laughed, as it has been written, 'hollowly'; the laugh of uneasiness rather than mirth.

Then he went and saw the lady.

She was waiting on a seat by a certain piece of water in Regent's Park. She must have had eyes behind, because, although she was sitting with her back to him, directly he stepped upon the grass she sprang up, and, as if she had been observing him all the time, went to him at something very like a run. He advanced at quick step. They met in the middle of the grass plot, contrary to regulations, which forbid people to walk upon the grass. They each gave two hands, and that with an air which suggested that if that had not been a public place they would have given each other something else as well.

'Guy!' she exclaimed. 'I thought you were the other side of the world. What a time you've been!'

'Coming from the other side of the world? or from Craven Street? It is some distance from Craven Street to Regent's Park.'

'You are in Craven Street, are you? What's it mean? You're looking well—sort of coppery colour; it suits you.'

'That's the air of the veldt; it burnishes a man's skin. You're looking sweet. I say, it's awfully hard lines that I can't kiss you. Mayn't I—just a little one?'

'In broad daylight, in Regent's Park, with a hundred pairs of eyes observing us from Hamilton Terrace? Thank you; some other day. When I had your note—what a note! "Meet me at the old place at noon"—I wondered who I was to meet, you or your ghost. As a matter of fact, I had a most important engagement—just at noon; but I put it off on purpose to come and see.'

'That was very dear of you. I'm not my ghost, I'm me.'

'But—Guy, have you made your fortune? You didn't seem as if you were going to make it at quite such a rate when you wrote last.'

He shook his head.

'Came back with less in my pockets than when I left.'

'Then—what does it mean?'

'My uncle's dead.'

'Mr Burton?'

He nodded.

'Has he left you his money? Oh, Guy!'

'As to that, I can't say. At present I know nothing. The fact is, Letty, it's—it's a queer business. You won't laugh?'

'What at?'

'Well'—he held out an envelope—'if I hadn't found this letter awaiting me telling me of the old man's death, I should have accused myself of softening of the brain, or something of the kind. As it is, I believe I've had a vision.'

'A vision! You? Guy, fancy your discovering that there are visions about.'

'You're laughing at me now.'

'I'm doing nothing of the kind. How can you say such a thing? I'm the soul of gravity. Do I ever laugh?'

As a matter of fact, there was a twinkle in her eyes even as she spoke, which he perceived.

'All right; laugh it out. I don't mind. All I can say is that it's gospel truth, and seems queer enough to me, though I daresay it's extremely comic to anybody else.'

'What seems comic? You haven't said a word.'

'Let's find a seat, and I'll say a good many.'

They found a seat—not the one she had been sitting on, but one which was sheltered by a tree. It was, perhaps, because it was in the shade that they temporarily ignored the fact that they were yet in Regent's Park. They were still pretty close together when he began to tell his tale.

'On the 23rd of February I had had a long day in the open. It was broiling hot, and in the evening I was glad to get back under cover. As I sat at my tent door, too tired even to smoke, I saw, right in front of me, my uncle.'

'Your uncle? Mr Burton? Where was this?'

'Perhaps three hundred miles north of Buluwayo.'

'But—what was your uncle doing there?'

'I told you it was a queer business, and so it was. Let me try to explain. Straight in front of where I was sitting the plain stretched for heaven knows how many miles right away to the horizon. There were no buildings; scarcely a bush or a tree was to be seen; just the monotonous level ground. All at once I perceived, certainly within a hundred feet of where I was, a flight of steps.'

'A flight of steps?'

'Well, I had a sort of general idea that there was a building in connection, but my eyes were fixed upon the steps. I seemed to know them. There was a wide open door at top. I felt that I was well acquainted with what was on the other side of that door. On the steps my uncle was standing. Mind, I saw him as well as I see you, and, thank goodness, I can see you pretty well. I can't tell you what he wore, because I'm no hand at describing clothes; but I've an impression that he had on a suit of tweeds and a bowler hat. He was apparently lounging on the steps, watching the passers-by. He did not see me—of that I was sure. On a sudden someone else came towards him up the steps. He was a stranger to me, though I think I should know him if I saw him again. He was taller than my uncle, and, I imagine, younger. Anyhow, he was altogether a bigger and a stronger man. He had a walking stick in his hand, with a horn handle. Directly he got within reach, without, so far as I could judge, uttering a word of warning, with this stick he struck my uncle with all his force across the face. I suspect that my uncle had seen him coming before I did, and, for reasons of his own, had stuck to what he deemed his post of vantage on the steps, being unwilling to go and meet him, and ashamed to run away. That he was not so taken aback by the suddenness of the attack as I was I felt persuaded. He put out his hand to guard himself, and, I fancy, at the last moment was disposed to turn tail and flee. But it was too late. The blow got home. He staggered back and would have fallen had not the stranger gripped him with his left hand, and commenced to belabour him with the stick which he held with his right. People came streaming out of the open door above and up the steps from the street. My uncle made not the faintest attempt at resistance. When the people came close enough to hamper the free action of his arm, the stranger, giving his victim a push, sent him head foremost down the steps. In an instant the whole thing vanished.'

Mr Holland ceased. The lady had been regarding him with wide-open grey eyes.

'Guy!' she said.

'Wasn't it odd?'

'Odd? You must have been dreaming.'

'I was as wide awake as you are. It was a mirage, or vision, or something of the kind. The queerest part of it was that it was so amazingly real, and so near. When the thing had gone I kept asking myself why I hadn't jumped up and interfered. I could have got there in a dozen strides.'

'Then what happened?'

'I sat for a long time half dazed, half expecting the thing to come again, or to continue from the point at which it had left off. Then I went and told a man with whom I was chumming what I'd seen. He said the sun had got into my eyes, advised me to have a drink—made fun of it altogether.

But I knew better; and, as it turned out, I was haunted by my uncle all through the night.'

'Awake or sleeping?'

'Awake. I couldn't sleep. I was haunted by a feeling that he was dying. The stranger had not killed him; but in consequence of the thrashing he had received he was struggling with death, and kept calling out to me to come to him; and I couldn't.'

'Poor Guy!'

The lady softly stroked the hand of his which she held between her two.

'I wondered if I was on the verge of an attack of illness or going mad, or what, though personally I felt as fit as a fiddle all the time, with my senses as much about me as they are now. I kept hearing him call out, over and over again, "Guy, Guy!" in the voice I knew so well and wasn't particularly fond of. There was something else which he kept repeating.'

'What was that?'

'"The ruby."'

'The ruby?'

'I haven't a notion of what he meant or what the whole thing meant, but at least a dozen times that night I heard him referring to a ruby,—the ruby, he called it. Long and seemingly involved sentences I heard him utter, but the only two words I could distinguish were those two—"the ruby"; and, as I have said, those two I heard him pronounce certainly a dozen times. And in the morning I was conscious of an absolute conviction that he was dead.'

'How very strange.'

'I'm not one of your clever chaps, so I don't pretend to be able to suggest a sufficient explanation, but the entire business reminds me of what I've heard about second sight. Although in the body I was out there on the veldt I seemed to know and see what was taking place heaven knows how many thousand miles away. In spite of the persuasion which was borne in upon me that he was dead, every day, and sometimes all day, I heard him calling out to me, "Guy, Guy!" and every now and then, "The ruby!" It was as if he were imploring me to come to him.'

'So you came.'

'So I came. The truth is I couldn't stand it any longer. I should have gone off my head if I had had much more of it. I was good for nothing, my nerves were all anyhow, everyone was laughing at me. So I slipped off by myself without a word to a creature; got down to Cape Town, found a boat just starting, and was off on it at once. Directly the boat was away the haunting stopped. My nerves were all right in an instant. I told myself I was an ass; that I ought to have wired or written, or done something sensible. Since, however, it was too late I tried to make the best of things. I ran up to London so soon as we reached port, meaning, if it turned out that my imagination had made a fool of me, to go straight back without breathing a word to anyone of my ever having come.'

'Not even to me?'

'Not even to you. You wouldn't have liked me to turn up with nothing but a bee in my bonnet.'

'So long as you turned up, I shouldn't have cared for forty thousand bees. The idea!'

'That's very sweet of you. As it happened, no sooner did I appear at my old quarters than Mrs Flickers produced a letter which had arrived for me—she did not know how long ago, and which she had not known what to do with. It turned out to be an intimation from Collyer that that my uncle had died on the 23rd of February, the very day on which, out on the veldt, I had seen him assaulted by that unknown individual upon that flight of steps.'

'Guy, is this a ghost story you have been telling me? I don't want to be absurd, but it really does look as if it were a case of the hand of destiny.'

'I don't know about the hand of destiny, but it does look as if it were a case of something.'

'I shouldn't be surprised if, after all, the old reprobate has left you some of his money.'

'Nor I. Oh, Letty, if he has! We'll be married on Monday.'

'As this is Friday, couldn't you make it Sunday? Monday seems such a long way off. My dear Guy, first of all interview Mr Samuel Collyer. Then you'll learn the worst.'

'I am going to. Of course I had to see you first—'

'Of course.'

'But I wired to him that I'd call this afternoon.'

'Then call.'

And Mr Holland called.

CHAPTER II.
THE QUEST ORDAINED

Mr Collyer's offices were in Pump Court, first floor front. Mr Samuel Collyer was a somewhat short and pursy gentleman of about fifty years of age, with a clean-shaven face, and a manner which gave such a varying complexion to the words he used as to cause it sometimes to be very difficult to make out exactly what it was he meant; an extremely useful manner for a solicitor to have. As with alert, swinging stride Mr Holland entered, Mr Collyer rose, greeting him with his usual stolid air, as if he had just looked in from across the road, instead of from the wilds of Africa.

'Good morning, Mr Guy. You're looking very brown.'

'Yes, I—I'm feeling very brown.'

The words seemed to come from him almost before he knew it, on the spur of the moment, as if the presence of a third person lent them a special significance. Reclining in the only armchair the room contained was a young gentleman of about Mr Holland's own age. He was well dressed, good looking, very much at his ease, and he regarded Mr Holland with a suggestion of amusement which seemed somehow to be very much in character.

'In questions of feeling is brown the equivalent of blue?'

Mr Holland's bearing was not so genial as the other's.

'I did not expect to see you here.'

'Nor, my dear Guy, did I expect to see you. I did not even wish to.'

'That I can easily believe.'

'It is Mr Collyer's fault that I am here, not mine. I should have been content never to set eyes on you again; and as for being in the same room with you—'

He left his sentence unfinished, with a little airy movement of his hand, which seemed to round it off with a sting. He continued to smile, although Mr Holland regarded him for a moment with eyes which were very far from smiling. The newcomer turned to the solicitor.

'I have your letter.'

'I presume, Mr Guy, that you had my letter nearly three months ago.'

'I had it this morning. I only came back from Africa last night.'

'From Africa? I was not aware you had gone so far.'

'Dear Guy is such a gadabout.'

The interpolation came from the young gentleman in the arm-chair. The solicitor went on.

'The only address I had was the one in Craven Street. As my letter did not come back I supposed it had reached you safely; but that, for reasons of your own, you chose to take no notice of it. You know, Mr Guy, that in such matters you are a little erratic.'

'I know. You needn't remind me. So my uncle is dead. Of what did he die?'

'The immediate cause was apoplexy, brought on, it is to be feared, by something which happened on the afternoon of his decease.'

The young gentleman in the arm-chair struck in.

'He was thrashed within an inch of his life, and very properly he was served.'

'Thrashed! Where? On a flight of steps?'

'On the steps of the Hôtel des Anglais at Nice.'

'Good God! I thought I knew the place; of course it was the Hôtel des Anglais; it's—it's past believing.'

The solicitor misapprehended the cause of Mr Holland's excitement.

'It does seem almost incredible; none the less it is a lamentable fact.'

The young gentleman put in his word.

'How incredible? The dear man misbehaved himself with another man's wife, as was his invariable custom when he had a chance. The other man thrashed him for it. What could be more natural? or simpler?'

Mr Holland ignored the inquiry.

'What is it, Mr Collyer, which you wish to say to me?'

'It is not so much that I have anything to say to you as that I have a duty to perform. I have to read to you your uncle's will. His instructions were that it was to be read only in the presence of both his nephews, his sole remaining relatives.'

'He has probably left all his money to found a hospital for cats, and wished us both to be present, my dear Guy, so that we might enjoy each other's discomfiture.'

Mr Holland said nothing. Mr Collyer was taking some papers out of a metal box which stood against the wall, and on the front of which was painted in white letters the name, 'George Burton.' Reseating himself behind his table he held up a large white linen envelope, such as is used in England for registered letters.

'I will read you the endorsement which is on it. "This envelope, which he told me contained his will, was delivered to me by Mr George Burton, on the 22nd of June 1899, and was then and there sealed by me in the presence of my two clerks whose names are undersigned." Then follow my own signature, and the signatures of the clerks in question, both of whom are still in my employ, Ferdinand Murpeatt and Benjamin Davis. Would either of you gentlemen like to see them?'

'My good Mr Collyer, we don't want to see your clerks. Your clerks be sanctified. Why all this form and fuss? Make an end of it. Let's know if it's cats or dogs Uncle Burton's favoured.'

'And you, Mr Guy, are you content that I should proceed at once to the contents of this envelope?'

Mr Holland said nothing; he simply nodded. The solicitor, taking a penknife, began to cut open the top of the envelope with a degree of care which perhaps erred on the side of overcaution. He addressed them as he did so.

'I may say that, beyond Mr Burton's own statement that it holds his will, I have no notion what this envelope contains. I have no knowledge of the purport of the will; Mr Burton never gave me the faintest hint as to what were his testamentary intentions. You are aware that your uncle was a man who did what he liked, in his own way; and I say this, therefore, in order to give you to understand that whatever form the will may take, I am not to be held responsible.'

The young gentleman in the arm-chair laughed.

'My dear Collyer, do cut the cackle, and do let's come to the 'osses.'

Mr Collyer took out from the envelope a single sheet of paper. Without further preamble he commenced to read what was written on it, in a slow, monotonous, sing-song voice, as if it were something sacred which he almost felt it his duty to intone.

'"I, George Burton, of Hyde Park Terrace, London, W., do hereby announce that this is my last Will and Testament, as written with my own hand on June 17, 1899."'

'"I have only two relatives living, viz., my two nephews, Horace Burton, my brother's son, and Guy Holland, the son of my sister; and, since I love them equally well, I desire to do them equal justice."'

The reading was interrupted by prolonged laughter from the young gentleman in the arm-chair.

'The dear man!' he cried.

Mr Collyer continued.

'"I therefore give and bequeath all that I die possessed of, in real and personal estate, to my nephew, Guy Holland—"'

'Good Lord!' exclaimed the young gentleman in the arm-chair.

Mr Holland's lips might have been closed a little tighter. The lawyer went on unmoved.

'"Absolutely, to do with as he pleases, on condition that he recover from May Bewicke, the actress, whom he knows, my ruby signet ring, which she obtained from me by means of a trick on the 27th of this last May. The ring is well known to him, and to Horace, and to my lawyer, Samuel Collyer. The ring is to be delivered to Samuel Collyer, whom I hereby appoint my sole executor, by my nephew, Guy, within three months of the day of my death. Should he do so within the period mentioned, then I do hereby name him as my sole heir and residuary legatee. In default, however, of such delivery within the time stated, for any cause whatever, then my whole estate, without any deduction whatever, is to become the absolute property of my other nephew, Horace Burton."

"'Since the chances that Guy will obtain the ring from Miss Bewicke are not very large, that young woman preferring to keep tight hold of anything she has once laid her hands on, in making this will I am doing Horace even more than justice.'"

"'In the improbable case of the delivery of my ruby signet ring by Guy to Samuel Collyer, within the aforementioned three months of my decease, it is to be held by the said Samuel Collyer, and not to pass out of his possession until his death, when it is to be sold, and the proceeds devoted to form a Society for the Reformation of Actresses.'"

"'As witness my hand and signature this seventeenth day of June, Eighteen hundred and ninety-nine. George Burton.'"

"'Witnesses—'"

"'John Claney, 13 Porchester Terrace, W.'"

"'Augustus Evans, 83 Belgrave Row, S.W.'"

The reading was followed by silence, broken by a question from Mr Holland.

'And pray what is the plain English of it all?'

'The will is plain English. You are to obtain a certain ring from a certain lady and deliver it to me within a certain time. If you do so you are your uncle's heir; if you do not, Mr Horace is.'

'Within three months of his death. He died on the 23rd of February. This is the 19th of May. I have four days in which to get the ring.'

'Apparently that is the case.'

'Supposing this lady refuses to give me the ring when I ask for it, as, so far as I can perceive, she will be perfectly justified in doing.'

'Perfectly!'

The murmur came from Horace.

'How am I to get it from her within four days? Where is Miss Bewicke now?'

'In London. She is acting at the Modern Theatre. I am afraid I am unable to assist you with any advice as to how you are to procure the ring should she refuse to hand it over.'

Mr Holland stood up.

'Is that will a good one?'

'You mean in a legal sense. I should say so, perfectly. It is just the sort of will I should have expected your uncle to make. It is distinctly characteristic of the man.'

'My uncle was a most delightful person. Then, if I do not succeed in jockeying this lady out of her property inside four days I'm a pauper.'

'At least you will not inherit under your uncle's will.'

As Mr Holland stood with knitted brows his cousin gave him a friendly pat upon the back. Mr Holland whirled round to him in a manner which was distinctly not friendly.

'How dare you touch me, sir!'

'My dear Guy! May not a cousin give a cousinly salutation to a cousin? My congratulations, my dear boy. You're sure to be the heir. You always were so clever at diddling a woman.'

The blood showed even through Mr Holland's bronzed cheeks; his clenched fists twitched. The other, however, paid no heed to these signs and portents.

'I believe you managed to diddle Miss Bewicke once before, eh, Guy?' He turned upon his heels, with a little movement of his shoulders. 'Let's hope you'll succeed the second time as well as I've been given to understand you did the first. Good-bye. Good luck, dear boy. Collyer, I'll look in on you again.'

Mr Horace Burton strolled from the room. Presently Mr Holland followed him.

'I, also, Mr Collyer, will talk things over when I look in again. I don't feel equal to the task just now.' He said to himself as he was going down the stairs, 'Nice to have to rob your old sweetheart to keep yourself out of the gutter. He knew very well there had been passages between us; so he set me the dirtiest job to do which he could think of. The brute!

21

I'd better have stayed in Africa than have come back to this. I wonder what Letty'll say.'

The solicitor, left alone, leaning back in his chair, stroked his chin with his hand as if to discover whether it wanted shaving.

'They don't know that Miss May Bewicke is Mr Samuel Collyer's niece. I fancy that there are only one or two persons who are aware that he has a niece upon the stage. George Burton certainly was not.'

He smiled as if his own thoughts tickled him.

CHAPTER III.
MISS BROAD COMMANDS

They were in Regent's Park again; at the same place; on the same seat. She said to him as he came up,—

'I told papa that you were here. I'm of age, and I suppose I'm entitled to do as I please; but I made up my mind that I'd have no secrecy. It's degrading.'

'Well, degrading's strong. And what did papa say?'

'I mentioned, at the same time, that your uncle was dead, and under the circumstances he perhaps thought it advisable not to say much. At anyrate he didn't.'

'He might have done; and he will do soon.'

Something in his tone caught her ear.

'Guy! What's the matter? You don't mean—?'

'Not exactly, though I'm not sure it isn't worse.'

She half rose from the seat.

'Has he left you nothing?'

He told her the purport of his uncle's will; she listening eager-eyed and open-mouthed.

'Do you mean to say that you're to get this ridiculous ring out of Miss Bewicke's possession in four days, by fair means or foul?'

He nodded.

'But it's monstrous.'

'It is a pretty tall order?'

'What do you propose to do?'

'I propose to call upon Miss Bewicke.'

In a moment, without any warning, she was standing up beside him stiff and straight.

'I see. Now I understand. That's the Idea. I've no doubt that Miss Bewicke will find you a most persuasive person.'

'My dear Letty!'

'Weren't you and Miss Bewicke once engaged to be married? Pray don't trouble yourself to explain. I know all about it. You need have no fear of losing your uncle's inheritance. You are quite sure to understand each other. She'll be delighted to give you the ring in exchange for another. Would you like to give her mine?'

She actually began to unbutton her glove. He groaned.

'It's worth while seeing ghosts in Africa for this!'

'And what do you propose to say to Miss Bewicke when you call upon her?'

'That's what I want you to tell me.'

'I tell you! As if you didn't know! After the stories I have heard of her I had hoped that you would have had no more to do with Miss Bewicke. But, of course, my wishes do not count.'

'If the stories you have heard are to Miss Bewicke's discredit, you may take my word for it that they are libels.'

'You are sure to know. I am glad you have such a high opinion of her. When you have seen her you might let me know what she says. That is, if she should say anything which was not spoken in the strictest confidence.'

She actually walked away. He went after her.

'My dear Letty, don't you want me to try to get the ring?'

'By all means act in accordance with the dictates of your better judgment. You are so much wiser than I.'

'But, Letty, if I don't get the ring, I—I won't say I lose you, because God knows I hope I never shall do that; but it means that I shall have to wait for you, the Powers above alone can tell how long. While getting it means getting you at once.'

'Guy, weren't you once engaged to be married to Miss Bewicke?'

'Yes, I was.'

'And I suppose you loved each other?'

'Letty, it's not like you to rub it in like this.'

'My dear Guy, let us look the situation fairly in the face. This person, from whom you are going to ask this weighty favour—in effect you are going to ask her to bestow on you a fortune—is the woman whom once you loved, and who was once your promised wife. I don't like it; it's no use pretending to you that I do.'

'My dear Letty, do you think I like it? If it weren't for circumstances I'd let the ruby and the fortune go together. Listen, the decision shall be in your hands. Shall I try to fulfil the old man's preposterous and malignant condition? or shall I throw the whole thing up at once, let the money go to Horace Burton, return to Africa, and keep on pounding away in the hope of making enough to win you in the end? Now, which is it to be? You shall say.'

'It's not fair to place the entire responsibility upon my shoulders.'

'Since this is a matter in which you are primarily interested, my one desire is that your views should be treated with the utmost possible deference.'

'Then get the ruby.'

'But how?'

'Tear it from her if you like; knock her down and steal it; I don't care. Only don't make love to her under the pretence of doing me a service. Guy, if you're even civil to her—'

She left the sentence unfinished; the air with which she spoke was eloquent enough.

'My dear Letty, as if I should! Then do you suggest that I should go and see her?'

'Of course. To-night.'

'To-night?'

'At once. And get the ruby from her somehow; I don't care how, but get it. And meet me here in the morning with it in your hand.'

'But, dearest, Miss Bewicke goes to the theatre.'

'I don't care where she goes.'

'Exactly, but I can hardly interview her in the theatre; and, in any case, she would scarcely have the ruby with her there.'

'Then see her after.'

'After the theatre?'

'Oh, Guy, don't keep asking me questions! If you only knew how I hate the notion of your seeing her at all, especially to solicit a favour at her hands. But since I suppose you must, you must get it over. Only I know what took place between you before; papa knows and everybody knows—heaps of people have told me.' A curious something came into her voice, a sort of choking sound. It frightened Mr Holland. 'Guy, you must see her to-night—to-night—and never again. Get the ruby from her if you have to fight her for it, and meet me here to-morrow morning with it in your hand.'

Without a word of warning she scurried from him down the path. He called after her.

'Letty!'

'Don't try to stop me. I don't want to speak to you when you're going to see that woman.'

There was that in her voice which caused him to deem it advisable to take her at her word. He let her go. He remained behind to objurgate fickle fortune and other things. He told himself, not for the first time,—

'It really was not worth while to see ghosts in Africa for this. If spectral visitations all tend this way I bar them. The next ghost I see I'll decline to notice it. It shall lead somebody else into a mess, not me.' He began to stroll towards the gate, kicking every now and then at the pebbles on the path. 'Never thought Letty was such a little spitfire. Bless her heart! I love her for it all the more. Who can have told her about the mess I made of things with May? I'll swear I didn't. These things will out.' He groaned. 'It's past seven. I'll go and get something to eat. Then if food screws my courage to the sticking point I'll go and interview Miss Bewicke a little later. But as for taking that ruby from her *vi et armis*—oh, lord! If ever there was a forlorn hope, I'm down for one to-night.'

Miss Bewicke had a flat in Victoria Street. A little after half-past eleven Mr Holland addressed himself to the hall porter with an inquiry if she was in. There was that in his bearing which suggested that the food which he had consumed had not exhilarated him to any appreciable extent. In fact, so melancholy was his air that one would not have been surprised to learn that it had injuriously affected his digestion. The porter regarded him askance.

'Do you know Miss Bewicke?'

'I have that honour.'

'Sure?'

'Tolerably sure.'

'You'll excuse my asking you, but such a lot of people, perfect strangers, come hanging about and annoying her that my orders are not to let anybody go up if I can help it who isn't a friend of hers. I understand you to say that you are a friend.'

'A friend of some years' standing.'

Mr Holland sighed. The porter observed him with dubious glances, being possibly doubtful as to the meaning of the sigh.

'I suppose it's all right if you're a friend of hers; you ought to know best if you are. I can only say that you'll do no good if you're trying it on. I don't know if Miss Bewicke is in; I don't think she's returned from the theatre. But you can go up and see. I'll take you up in the lift if you like.'

The porter took him up in the lift. On the way Mr Holland asked a question.

'Do Miss Bewicke's unknown admirers allow their admiration to carry them as far as her private residence?'

'I don't know about admiration. Idiots I call them; and sometimes worse. People hang about here all day, and sometimes half the night, trying to introduce themselves to her, and I don't know what rubbish. Why, I've known half-a-dozen cabs follow her from the theatre to the very door.'

'Empty cabs?'

'Not much; a fool, and sometimes two fools, in each.'

'Ah!' Mr Holland reflected. 'If Miss Bewicke had been destined to be my wife I wonder how I should have enjoyed her being the object of such ardent admiration. Under such circumstances a husband's feelings must be worth dissection.'

In reply to Mr Holland's modest knock, the door of Miss Bewicke's apartments was opened by a young gentleman well ever six feet high, who appeared to be in rather a curious frame of mind.

'What the deuce do you want?' was his courteous salutation.

'I want Miss Bewicke.'

'Oh, you do, do you? then just you come inside.'

He took Mr Holland by the shoulder, and that individual, although a little surprised at the young gentleman's notion of the sort of reception which it was advisable to accord a friendly visitor, suffered him to lead him to an apartment which was beyond. This was apparently a sitting-room, prettily furnished, particularly with photographs, as is the manner of ladies who are connected with the theatre, and contained a table which was laid for two. The young gentleman still did not release Mr Holland's shoulder. He glared at him instead, and put to him this flattering question,—

'Are you the blackguard who has been making himself a nuisance about the place this last week and more?'

Mr Holland's reply was mild in the extreme.

'I hope not.'

'You hope not? What do you mean by that? Don't you know you are?'

'I do not. I think the mistake, sir, is yours. May I ask who you are? You have your own ideas of how to greet the coming guest. Does Miss Bewicke keep you on the premises in order that you may mete out this kind of treatment to all her friends? You should be popular.'

'You're no friend of Miss Bewicke's. Don't try to bounce me, sir. I'll tell you in two words who I am. My name's Dumville—Bryan Dumville. Miss Bewicke is shortly to be my wife. As her affianced husband I consider myself entitled to protect her from the impertinent attentions of any twopenny-ha'penny bounder who chooses to think that because she condescends to appear upon the stage of a theatre he is at liberty to persecute her when and how he pleases.'

'Your sentiments do you credit, Mr Dumville.'

'Don't try to soft-soap me, sir. You can speak smoothly enough to me; but I will give you ten seconds, before I throw you down the stairs, to explain the meaning of your presence here.'

'I think, Mr Dumville, that, if I were you, I should make it a little more than ten seconds before, as you put it, you throw me down the stairs. I have come to see Miss Bewicke. I am afraid I can only explain myself to her.'

'No, you don't. That trick's been played before! It's stale; out you go!'

'Don't be an ass, sir!'

'Ass!'

The epithet seemed to add fuel to the excitable Mr Dumville's flame. Throwing both arms round Mr Holland, trying to lift him off the ground, he proceeded to hustle him towards the door. Mr Holland, unwilling to be treated in quite such unceremonious fashion, displayed a capacity for resistance for which, possibly, the other was unprepared. There was every prospect of a delightful little bout of rough and tumble, when an interruption came.

'Bryan! what are you doing?'

The interruption came from a young lady who was standing at the open door.

CHAPTER IV.
MR HOLLAND FAILS

A Small young lady, daintily fashioned, with a child-like face. She was charmingly dressed; a big feather boa was round her neck. As she stood there, in spite of the perfection of her attire, she looked more like a child than a woman. The men released each other. Mr Dumville explained.

'I was only going to throw the fellow down the stairs.'

'Is that all? And what has'—there was a little hesitation; then the word was softened by a smile—'the fellow done? And who may the fellow be?'

'I don't know. Some bounder, I suppose.'

Mr Dumville seemed slightly disconcerted, as if the situation had not quite shaped as he had expected. Mr Holland's hat and stick had fallen to the floor. He stooped to pick them up. When he turned there came an exclamation from the little lady at the door.

'Guy!'

'Miss Bewicke.'

'Whoever would have thought of seeing you? Why, this is Mr Holland, a friend of my childish days.'

She advanced with a tiny gloved hand held out to him. Mr Dumville, whose hands were in his trouser pockets, seemed disposed to be grumpy.

'It wasn't my fault; he should have told me.'

'You hardly gave me an opportunity.'

'My dear Bryan, I believe you're a little mad; that is, I believe you're a little madder even than I thought you were. Guy, this is Bryan Dumville, a gentleman who thinks that he has claims on me. Bryan, this is Guy Holland, who was a friend of mine when I was quite a little child; and that—how long ago that is!'

'I don't see how I'm to blame. The porter was talking about the fellow who has been such a nuisance, saying that he has been making himself particularly objectionable to-day, trying to force his way upstairs, and I don't know what; and he added that he was hanging about at that very moment, and if he turned his back he shouldn't be surprised if the blackguard made another try to get at you. I made up my mind that if he did I would give him what for. So, when someone knocked at the door, and I found it was a man, I went for him.'

'Nothing could be more natural.'

If Mr Holland's tone was a little dry Mr Dumville did not seem to notice it; but the lady regarded the speaker with laughter lighting all her pretty face.

'Guy, you must sup with us.'

'Thank you, I have not long dined.'

'That doesn't matter; you must eat with us again.' She rang the bell. A maid appeared. 'Bring another plate; Mr

Holland will join us at supper.' Miss Bewicke proceeded to remove her outdoor things, handing them to Mr Dumville one by one, talking as she did so. 'Someone told me that you were at the other side of the world—at the North Pole, I think.'

'Not the North Pole; but I have been to Africa. I only returned last night.'

'And you came to-day to see me? How perfectly delightful of you.'

Mr Holland winced. He was conscious that the lady might misapprehend the situation.

'The fact is, I have something rather important which I wish to say to you.'

'Indeed? How interesting! I like people to say important things to me. Say it while we're at supper. That is, if it's something Bryan may be allowed to listen to.'

'If I'm in the way I'll go.'

Mr Holland was silent. He felt that Mr Dumville was in the way, but that he himself was hardly in a position to say so. Miss Bewicke spoke for him.

'My dear Bryan, when you're in the way we'll let you know. Now, people, will you please sit down?' They seated themselves at table. 'What is this very important thing?—must it out?—or will it keep?'

Mr Holland reflected. He thought of Letty, and other things. Miss Bewicke seemed disposed to be friendly. Perhaps it was as well there was a third person present. He decided to make the running.

'It's this way. My uncle's dead.'

'Your uncle? Mr George Burton? I hope you won't think me dreadful, but I cannot say I'm sorry. He was not a person for whom I entertained feelings of profound respect.'

'He—he's left rather a peculiar will.'

'I'm not surprised. I should be surprised at nothing he did which was peculiar. I never knew him do anything which wasn't. Or worse.'

Mr Holland resolved to plunge.

'He says you have a ruby ring of his.'

'He says?—who says?'

'My uncle—in his will.'

Miss Bewicke laid down her knife and fork. 'Mr Holland, do I understand that you intend to suggest that I have in my possession another person's property?'

'It's like this. He had a ruby ring, I know it very well. In his will he says you have it. He may have given it to you for all I know; he did queer things—'

'Thank you.'

'I don't mean that.'

'It doesn't matter. Go on.'

'Anyhow, it's a condition of his will that I'm to get it back from you, and if I don't get it back within three months of his death I'm to lose his money.'

36

'I don't in the least understand you. Will you please be so good as to make yourself quite clear.'

He made himself as clear as he could, though he did not find it easy. Nor was his explanation well received.

'Then am I to gather that you have come to me at midnight, hot-foot from Africa, in order to get from me—a ring; a ruby ring?'

'It doesn't sound very nice, but that's the plain truth of it.'

'It's very flattering.'

'Very!'

The chorus came from Mr Dumville, and was accompanied by a glare.

'I can only throw myself upon your mercy, Miss Bewicke, and implore you to let me have this ring to save my inheritance.'

Miss Bewicke resumed her knife and fork, which had all this time been lying idle. There was a change in her manner, which, though subtle, was well defined to Mr Holland's consciousness.

'By the way, Mr Holland, the other day I heard your name associated with a person called, I think, Broad. Was it merely idle gossip, or do you know anything of a person with a name like that?'

'I do. I know Miss Broad, and very well. I hope she will be my wife. She has promised that she will.'

'Ah, you and I know what is the value of such promises, don't we, Mr Holland? Is she any relation to Broad, the teaman, in Mincing Lane?'

'She is his daughter; his only child.'

'Indeed! His only child? How delightful! Old Broad has bushels of money. How nice for you, of all men, to be received in such a family.'

The airy insolence of the tone was meant to sting, and did, though he endeavoured to conceal the fact.

'You haven't answered my question.'

'Haven't I? What was your question?'

'Will you let me have the ring, to save my inheritance?'

'It's such an odd question—isn't it, Bryan? So mysterious. Melodrama's not at all my line. They say I'm too small. Do you think that I'm too small?'

'I should imagine that you were better fitted to shine in domestic comedy.'

His words conveyed a meaning which this time stung her, although she laughed.

'But, my dear Mr Holland, what do you want with an inheritance when you are going to marry a rich wife—the only child of her father, and he a widower. I'm told that old Broad's a millionaire.'

'I'm not marrying her for her father's money; nor for her own. Nor do I intend to go to her empty-handed.'

'How chivalrous you are! So changed!'

'Am I to have the ring?'

'Really, Mr Holland, you speak to me as if it were a case of stand and deliver. You can hardly know how your uncle behaved or I do not think you would broach the subject to me at all. In any case it is not one which I can discuss with you. Talk it over with Mr Dumville. Whatever he wishes I will do. I always act on his advice; he is so very wise. Goodnight, Mr Holland. So glad to have seen you. Come soon again. Goodnight, Bryan, dear.'

'But you haven't had any supper.'

'Mr Holland has taken my appetite away; he has caused my mind to travel back to events which I am always endeavouring to forget. But it doesn't matter. Hear what he has to say, and decide for me. King will let you both out when your discussion's finished.'

Mr Holland stood up.

'Miss Bewicke, I am very sorry if I have said anything which has given you pain or offence. Nothing could have been further from my intention.'

'Thank you.'

'But this matter which you treat so lightly—'

'Lightly!'

'Is to me almost one of life and death. I believe that my uncle has left something like a quarter of a million.'

'What a sum, Bryan! Doesn't it sound nice?'

'If I can hand this ring to Mr Collyer—'

'To whom?'

'To Mr Collyer, my uncle's solicitor, the money is mine. I have only four days left to do it in.'

'Four days! Just now you said three months.'

'The time appointed is three months after my uncle's death. He died on the 23rd of February. I have only just become acquainted with the terms of his will. So in four days it will be decided if I am to be a rich man or a pauper. You see, Miss Bewicke, that my fate is in your hands.'

'I really cannot discuss the matter with you now. It would make me ill. The strain would be too much for me. I refer you to Mr Dumville. Bryan, dear, I leave the matter entirely in your hands.'

'Miss Bewicke—'

Mr Dumville rose.

'Mr Holland, you have heard what Miss Bewicke has said. So far as she is concerned the discussion is closed. My dear, let me open the door for you.'

He opened the door for her. She passed out, with her handkerchief to her eyes. A fact on which Mr Dumville commented.

'You see what you have done, sir—affected her to tears.'

'To what?'

'To tears!'

'Oh!'

'Well, sir, what have you to say to me?'

'To you?'

'Yes, sir, to me. You have said more than enough to Miss Bewicke. Now, perhaps there is something which you would like to say to me, as her affianced husband.'

'There are one or two things which I should like to say to you, but I am inclined to think that I had better not say them to you here. Nor do I quite see my way to ask you to come outside, though I should like to.'

Mr Holland was savage, and unwise enough to show it. Mr Dumville, having polished his eyeglass, replaced it in his eye so that he might scan the speaker with a greater show of dignity.

'What on earth do you mean by talking to me like that? If that's the kind of remark you wish to make the sooner you get away the better.'

'I am quite of your opinion, Mr Dumville. I shall always remember with pleasure that I was able to get away from you.'

Mr Dumville strode forward.

'You be hanged, sir!'

'After you, Mr Dumville, after you.'

'You had better be careful; although I don't want to have a vulgar row with you here.'

'Would you mind mentioning a place at which you would? I will try to make it convenient to be there.'

Mr Dumville turned and rang the bell.

'What's that for?'

'For the servant to show you out.'

Mr Holland laughed, showing himself out without another word. He was conscious of two things—that he had not been particularly discreet, and that he would like to make his indiscretion greater by 'taking it out' of somebody. It was not often his temper gained the upper hand; when it did he was apt to be dangerous both to himself and others.

Nor was his mood chastened by a little incident which took place as he was about to descend the staircase. From a door which opened behind him Miss Bewicke addressed him in mellifluous accents.

'Oh, Mr Holland, will you give my fondest love to dear Miss Broad? It's true that I don't know her, but if you tell her what good friends you and I used to be I'm sure that she won't mind. I hope to make her acquaintance one of these days, and then I'll tell her how fond you and I were of one another. Good-night.'

Before he had a chance to answer the door was closed. He went down the stairs in a rage.

'The little cat!' he muttered. 'The little cat! who would have thought she had such claws?'

As he was going out into the street a woman, running against him, almost knocked him over. She was entering the house, apparently in hot, unseeing haste; putting up her hand as if to prevent his observation of her features; flying up the stairs as if danger was hard upon her heels.

Mr Holland adjusted his hat, which she had knocked almost off without offering the least apology.

'I wonder what mischief you have been up to? Women are beauties, real beauties!'

Having indulged himself in this very cheap piece of cynicism, he, metaphorically, shook the dust of the house from off his feet, but had not gone a dozen paces when he found himself face to face with his cousin, Horace Burton.

CHAPTER V.
A WOMAN SCORNED

Mr Burton might have been awaiting Mr Holland. He did not seem at all surprised to see him there, even at that hour of the night, or, rather, morning, for midnight had long since chimed.

'How do, dear boy? So you haven't been letting the grass grow under your feet. That's where you beat me; you are so energetic.'

And Mr Burton smiled. That smile was his most prominent feature. It was always there. Not that it necessarily denoted mirth. Not at all. It might mean anything, or nothing. When he was in a rage he smiled, and when he was in the best of tempers; when he wished to be agreeable, and when he wished to be nasty—and he could be nasty. He was not a bad-looking man, in his way, though there was something about him a little suggesting the worst side of the Semite, which rather detracted from the general effect. It was difficult to say exactly what it was. Whether it was that his nostrils were unduly thick, or that so much of his mouth as his heavy moustache suffered to be visible was animal, or that his eyes, which were fine of their kind, had an odd trick of intently observing you when you were not looking at him, and of wandering away into space when you were, it would have needed an acute physiognomist to determine, and then that physiognomist might have been in error. Certainly there was something about Mr Horace Burton which nearly always caused an experienced man of the world, on first making his acquaintance, to glance at him a first, a second, and again a third time, and then start thinking. Perhaps it was that, in spite of his moustache, his chronic smile displayed his teeth, which were not nice ones; or because of his soft, purring voice, which, when he became excited, had a squeak in it; or because of his feline trick of touching a person, with whom he might be conversing, with his fingertips, and stroking him, when he got near enough to do it.

Mr Holland regarded his cousin in silence. The encounter did not appear to astonish him, nor to add to his pleasure either. Mr Burton continued.

'Well—have you got it?'

'Have I got what?'

'Ah—you've answered. You haven't. I see. Thanks. It was rather sharp work to raid the girl at this hour of the night, don't you think? But you always were so keen. Was she nice to you? She used to be, didn't she? You've been a lucky chap. I never could make out what women saw in you to like. A lot of them have seen something. There's Miss Broad, for instance—'

'Don't mention that lady's name.'

'Not mention her name? My dear chap!' Mr Burton placed the finger-tips of his right hand against Mr Holland's chest, to have them brushed aside as if they were some noxious insect. He went on unmoved. 'She's to be my cousin; so I'm told. Unless you've jerked her up. I hear her father kicked you out of the house, perhaps you anticipate more kicking; in a case like that you can't kick back again. So perhaps you're wise to chuck the girl. I tell you what, dear boy.' The finger-tips returned, again to be displaced. 'Marry the Bewicke girl. Get a special license to marry the girl out of hand. Then you'll get the ruby and the money too. It's the only way you will. Hearken to the words of a wise man.'

'Mr Burton, although I am so unfortunate as to be a relative of yours, I have on a previous occasion been compelled to inform you that I decline to hold communication with, or afford you recognition of any sort or kind. I repeat that intimation now. With my reasons you are well acquainted; their name is Legion. Have the goodness, therefore, to let me pass.'

'But, my dear Guy, how about our uncle's money?'

'What about my uncle's money?'

'Our uncle's; forgive the plural, Guy. Hadn't we better come to some friendly arrangement while there still is time. You'll never get the ruby out of the Bewicke woman; I know her; she's a daughter of the horse-leech; she'll see you damned first. Relinquish the chase at once—you'll have to in a few hours, anyhow—and throw yourself on my magnanimity. There's a suggestion, Guy! Give it up; withdraw at once from what you know is a lost game, and I'll present you with a thousand pounds. Push the thing through to the bitter end, and you'll get nothing.'

'A thousand?—out of a quarter of a million?'

'It would be a gift, Guy—a free gift. It isn't every man who'd present a cousin who'd used him as you've used me with a free gift of a thousand pounds.'

'Mr Burton, if the money is to be yours, I'll have none of it. I'm not disposed to be beholden to your charity, nor to you in any way, as you are aware. If it is to be mine, you'll have none of it; I know your tastes, and will not pander to their gratification. Let me pass.'

'See how different we are. If the money is to be mine— and it will be; it's as good as mine already—I'll give you a few coppers every time we meet; I'll even send you some occasionally through the post. Good-night! My love to both the ladies!'

Mr Burton hailed a passing hansom and was driven off. Mr Holland continued his promenade, but had not gone far before he was accosted from behind.

'Mr Holland! Mr Holland!' exclaimed a female voice, as if the speaker were in distress for want of breath.

'Who's that?' He turned to see. A feminine figure was hastening towards him. 'This promises to be a night of adventure. Has that little hussy become humanised and changed her mind?'

The caller approached, holding her hand to her side.

'I wish to speak to you. You know me?'

They stood close to a lamp. Mr Holland looked her up and down.

'I seem to have seen you before. You are the person who rushed into the house as I came out.'

'That is it; I rushed—from him!'

She threw out her hand with a dramatic gesture, pointing down the street.

'From whom?'

'From your cousin—from Mr Horace Burton. Oh, he is a nice fellow! If I had stayed with him much longer I should have killed him; so to save myself from killing him I rushed away.'

'My cousin's concerns are not mine. I cannot assume responsibility for anything he may do or have done. You are mistaken if you suppose I can.'

'I am not mistaken; I know all that. You men are all the same; you hang together. If your own brother drives a woman into the gutter, you say it is no affair of yours; you pass on, you leave her there. Before you open your mouth I know you cannot be responsible for what he has done. But you can make me to be revenged on him.'

'Even that I cannot do.'

'You can! I say you can!'

The woman spoke, not loudly, but with such passion and intensity of meaning that Mr Holland was conscious of a curious sensation as he heard her. She was tall and thin, about thirty, not bad looking, but precisely the type of woman the ordinary rake, seeking for a victim, would, if he had his senses about him, have left severely alone. She was distinctly not a person to be trifled with. Apparently a foreigner, because, although she spoke fluent English, there was now and then a slight accent and a curious idiom which betrayed her. Written large all over her was what, to a practised eye, was unmistakable evidence that she was of the number of those who take all things seriously, even rakes. One could easily believe that to her a promise was a promise, though it came from the mouth of a man; and since there are men who regard promises made to women as a sort of persiflage, one would have thought that gentlemen who take that standpoint would carefully avoid an individual who eyed matters of the kind from such an inconveniently different point of view. Mr Horace Burton, however, was in some respects an unusual specimen even of his class. Possibly the consciousness that he ran the risk of burning his own fingers by playing tricks with this particular fire was the lure which drew him on.

Anyhow, Mr Holland told himself that this time his cousin had caught a Tartar, and became more and more convinced of it as the woman went on.

'My name is Louise Casata; I am Corsican, as he will find, your cousin. I am the companion of Miss May Bewicke.' Mr Holland pricked up his ears at this, which the woman, with her keen instinct, perceived. 'Now do you not remember me? I was with her when you used to make love to her. I used to think you did it very well. But in those days you were fond of her. Now it is of another woman you are fond. Although you may have forgotten, do not believe she has.'

This time Mr Holland winced.

'I think that now I do remember you. You used to write letters for her and that kind of thing.'

'All sorts of kinds of things. I do everything she tells me to; I am a Jack-of-all-trades. I would act for her one day; I can act, but I am too large a size. But that does not matter; nor does it matter what your cousin has done to me, though you can guess. But you cannot guess how he has lied and juggled.'

'I think I can.'

'Then you must know him very well. In which case you have my sympathy. What does matter is what you are going to do to him.'

'I am going to do nothing to him.'

'We will see; you will see; they all will see. Be still! Let me speak. He has told me about your uncle's will—about the ruby which Miss Bewicke has. How, if you get it from her, you are to have all the money; how, if you don't, he is to have it all. I know! Very well; you will get the ruby. That's what you will do to him. He will be ruined, body and soul; though, for his soul, that was lost long ago. If he wishes to keep his body out of prison he will have to be quick out of England. He will not find it easy. There are those who are watching for him too well.'

'Are you sure of what you say?'

'Am I sure! Do I not know? It is only because they think he will get his uncle's money that he has not been in prison before. I tell you there is a convict's uniform waiting for him in more than one place. You will fit it on his back. I shall be revenged. I will go and see him when he is in gaol. Every three months he will be allowed to receive a visit. I will be his visitor. To see me will give him pleasure. I shall have such nice things to say. Oh, yes!'

Mr Holland shivered. There was that about this woman which filled him with a sense of vague discomfort.

'I don't like your way of putting things at all!'

'What does it matter what you like? To get the ruby— that is your affair.'

'How do you suggest that I am, as you phrase it, "to get the ruby"?'

'You will have to take it.'

'Take it?'

'She will never give it to you—never. She hates you. She also has been looking for revenge. Now she has her chance. You behaved badly to her. Now she will behave badly to you.'

'I deny that I behaved badly to her. If you were acquainted with all the facts you would not judge me with such hard judgment.'

'She thinks that you behaved badly to her, and, for a woman, that is enough.'

'Then am I to take it that you only think that Horace Burton has behaved badly to you?'

The woman favoured him with a look which made him realise more clearly than anything which had gone before what a Tartar his cousin had encountered. She was silent for a moment or two. When she did speak, she spoke quietly; but it was a quietude in which there was a quality which was not peace.

'You think to get me in a rage. I am not such a fool. When I am in earnest I am not so easily angered. It is no affair of yours if it is only that I think he has treated me badly. It is your affair to get the ruby; and I tell you that to get it you must take it.'

'I am so dull as not to understand what you mean when you say that I must take it.'

'I will make it clear. You have four days—four only. Good! At one o'clock to-morrow night you will come to Miss Bewicke's rooms. She will be out. It is Saturday. She goes by the midnight train to Brighton until Monday. All will be dark. The front door you will find open. You will have but to push it to enter. You will go to her bedroom; it is in front of you, the second door on the right as you go in. That door, also, will be open. The dressing-table is before the window on the left. It has many little drawers. In them are a great number of her jewels. In the bottom little drawer on the right-hand side facing the glass there is one thing only; it is your uncle's ruby signet ring. I know. I have seen it very often. She is not proud of the way in which she got it; she calls it "old Burton's scalp." It is to her a trophy which she won in battle, so she keeps it all by itself in that little bottom drawer. You have but to put your hand in; it is yours. You go away; you close the doors behind you; for you the game is won.'

Mr Holland stared. The matter-of-fact air with which the proposal was made almost took his breath away.

'You are suggesting that I should commit burglary.'

She made a contemptuous movement with her head and hands.

'It is but a word; what does it matter—a word? It is a burglary of which you will hear nothing more. I promise you that Miss Bewicke will do nothing.'

53

'And the morality of the proceeding, what of that?'

'Morality!' She laughed. 'The morality! Do not talk to me such nonsense! Bah! As if anyone cared for morality except for the sake of a———. But I shall not contend with you; you but amuse yourself. You understand what I have said?'

'Perfectly. Too well.'

'Very good. Then I shall see you to-morrow night at one o'clock.'

'You will do nothing of the kind.'

'No, I shall not see you, because it will be dark; but you will be there. You will find the doors open, and everything as I have said. It is already late; I must go. Good-bye.'

She went, fluttering from him up the street at a gait which was half walk, half run. He stood looking after her, a little taken aback by the abruptness of her departure.

'That woman appears to have formed a high opinion of my character. She flatters me.'

CHAPTER VI.
MISS BROAD COMMANDS A SECOND TIME

The next morning, although he was early at the rendezvous, Miss Broad was there before him. He saw her before she saw him—or thought he did—and, unperceived, as he fancied, stood and watched her. She was reading a book, sitting a little sideways, so that he saw her profile clearly. It was a brilliant morning, and she was attired for the sun. She had on a light grey silky dress, which was covered with flowers, and a huge hat, about a yard round, which matched the dress. He thought how nice she looked. Of a charm so delicate. Instinct with the essence of all things spiritual. He had been depressed as he had come through the park. The mere sight of her dispelled the clouds. The blood moved brisker through his veins. Seeing how engrossed she was by what she read, thinking to take her by surprise, he began to steal towards her across the grass—which he ought not to have done. Hardly had he stepped over the little iron fence than a stentorian voice bawled,—

'Come out of that!'

The invitation was addressed to him, as others, including Miss Broad, perceived as well as he did. It was a keeper's civil method of suggesting that he should keep off the grass, which, just there, was fenced about. He bowed to Miss Broad with a feeble smile, she merely nodding in return, without rising from her seat. As he advanced towards her along the proper gravel path, he was a little conscious that his approach had been robbed of dignity. She received him with an air which was a little frigid—still without rising—and beginning at once on a subject which he would have liked postponed.

'Well? Have you got it?'

'Have I got what?'

'You know very well what I mean. Have you got the ruby?—as you promised.'

'As I promised? My dear Letty, I think that statement is—is a little unauthorised.'

'Does that mean that you haven't got it?'

'I'm afraid it does—as yet.'

'Did you try to get it?'

'I did.'

'Did you go and see that woman?'

'I called upon Miss Bewicke.'

'And do you mean to say that she refused to let you have it?'

'If you'll allow me, I'll tell you what took place.'

He told her—a trifle lamely, but still he presented her with a sufficiently clear picture of what actually occurred—sufficiently clear, that is, to inflame her with indignation. She listened with eyes which grew brighter and brighter, and lips which closed tighter and tighter. The spiritual side of her became less obvious.

'And do you mean to say that you allowed the creature to trample on you without a word of protest?'

'I am not aware that she did trample on me.'

'Not when, according to your own account, she treated you as if you were a dog? I wonder you didn't take her into your hands and strangle her.'

'My dear Letty!'

'Of course I don't mean that; but you know what I do mean. As for that man—that Mr What's-his-name—why didn't you knock him down?'

'In a lady's room? I did suggest that if he liked to step outside I should be happy to do him any little service which was in my power.'

'And what did he do?'

'Rang the bell and requested the servant to show me out.'

'And you went? You actually allowed this man to kick you out—for that was what it came to—without a word.'

'Well, my dear, Miss Bewicke called out to me as I was going down the stairs to say that she sent her love to you.'

'Guy! you dare to tell me such a thing? You allow that creature to insult me by sending such a message, or pretending to; and then you repeat her insolence to me. The little wretch! So you are ruined.'

'Not yet. There are still about four days between me and the worst.'

'Then do you propose to allow her to have you kicked out of her apartments on each of those four days? Besides insulting me? I had hardly imagined that you were that kind of person. But one learns. Well, I suppose if you don't mind, I needn't. Though I really think you might be better off if you returned to Africa before instead of afterwards.'

'That is something like the advice which Horace offered.'

She sat up straighter.

'Did you also see Mr Burton last night?'

'He was waiting in the street when I came out of Miss Bewicke's. He congratulated me on the result of my visit.'

'Really, you appear to have had a thoroughly enjoyable time. Everybody seems to have had a kick at you. For my part, Guy, rather than allow people to ride over me rough-shod, as you appear disposed to do, I'd—I'd—steal the ruby.'

'You are in accordance with still another piece of advice which I received.'

'Guy! what do you mean?' He told her of his interview with Miss Casata. When he had finished she drew a long breath.

'Guy, I should do as she says.'

'Letty!'

'I should, I really should. So long as you get the ruby, no matter what happens, you can't be worse off that you will be if you don't get it. If you don't get it, you are ruined. You will have to go back to Africa and stay there for the rest of your life, or, at anyrate, till both of us are old; because you know you've no more chance of getting money there than you have here, and that's none at all. And you know you promised papa, and I promised papa, that you wouldn't marry till you had money of your own. And that doesn't mean a pound or two; it means a lot. He doesn't like to think you're marrying me for his money.'

'Letty!'

'Well, he doesn't; you know he doesn't. Of course I know you're not, or should I be sitting here talking to you now? But papa's different. And, anyhow, we promised. If there was nothing else to be gained, I'd like you to take it if only for the sake of spiting that actress creature. I'll teach her to send me messages.'

'But, my dear Letty, I fancy you don't quite realise that you are suggesting that I should commit a felony.'

'Felony! Don't talk such stuff and nonsense.' Her words reminded him of some of Miss Casata's of the night before. For some cause he shivered. 'Doesn't your uncle as good as say she stole it from him? And didn't that woman tell you that she's ashamed of it herself, and that therefore she hides it away all alone in a drawer? That shows that she's perfectly conscious that it's as much your property as hers. Indeed, it's much more your property. Your uncle left it to you, and she's no right to keep you out of it a single moment. And she wouldn't, you know very well that she wouldn't, if it wasn't for me. You threw her over—'

'Pardon me, I did not.'

'Then did she throw you over?'

'That's nearer the mark.'

'Really, Guy, you have an agreeable way of commending yourself to me. Then am I to understand that she regards you as her cast-off rubbish?'

'We agreed that we had made a mistake. That is the truth of the matter. There was no throwing over on either side.'

'Now, Guy, I know more than you suppose. Do you mean to deny that she resents the idea of your being about to marry me?'

'She congratulated me on the fact last night.'

'Did she, indeed? How very good of her. And pray how did she congratulate you? As if she meant it?'

'I suppose she meant it.'

'You suppose! Do you dare to tell me that you don't know quite well that her congratulations were ironical?'

'Well, I confess I had my "doots."'

'There! Didn't I say so all along? Oh, Guy, how difficult it is to get things out of you. Now, try to be equally truthful again, and tell me, on your word of honour, if you don't know that she would give you the ruby without a moment's hesitation if it wasn't for me; that is, if the fact of our being engaged to each other didn't prevent you paying attention to her?'

'I shouldn't like to put it in that way; but I think it possible that Miss Bewicke might prove more malleable if the circumstances were other than they are.'

'Precisely. That is what I mean. So promise me that to-night you will take your own.'

'My own! Letty!'

'Promise me!'

'But, my dear Letty—'

'Of course there is an alternative. You can throw me over. We, in our turn, can agree that we have made a mistake. Then you will be able to make yourself agreeable to her; and you will be able to get the ruby that way.'

'But, my dear Letty, if you will only be reasonable—'

'It is you who are unreasonable. You allow an idea to mar our lifelong happiness. Before you realise how hollow it is it will be too late. There will be nothing in front of us but dreary years of waiting. You let the cup of happiness be dashed from your hand even when it is already at your lips. I release you, Guy. I will not be a clog on you, perhaps through all eternity.'

Her tone was sombre, funereal. Mr Holland groaned.

'Oh, Lord! Your logic is as beautiful as you are. It really was worth while seeing ghosts in Africa for this!'

She stood up.

'Then go back to Africa and see some more. You shall not stay here to laugh at me. Goodbye.'

He caught her by the hand.

'Letty! How can you be so cruel.'

'Then you should do as I ask you. As you would do, without hesitation, if you really had a spark of the love you pretend to have for me.'

'I will; I'll do whatever you ask, though I'm ashamed of myself when I say so.'

'Promise that to-night you'll take your own?'

'I promise.'

She sat down again, and was as nice as she could be; he only knew how nice that was. He would have been as happy as is possible if it had not been for the thoughts which were at the back of his head, and the prospect which lay in front of him.

Unfortunately, nearly all the time Miss Broad was causing him to realise his good fortune in winning the love of such a girl as she was he was picturing himself stealing up a flight of darkened stairs, like a thief.

CHAPTER VII.
THE BOTTOM DRAWER

That night he realised his own picture.

One o'clock was the hour suggested by Miss Casata. Twenty times before that hour arrived he told himself that he had better return to Africa—ghosts or no ghosts—than do this thing. It seemed to him that dishonour hedged him round about; that whichever way he went he would find himself among the thorns. If he did this thing he would break his plighted word; quite possibly lose his love and his fortune too. If he did the other he might quite possibly find himself up to the neck in a slough of misunderstandings—to speak of nothing worse—from which he could never emerge as clean as he went in. The choice was a pleasant one. Yet he never hesitated as to which horn of the dilemma he would thrust himself on. Although very much against his will, he was set on burglary. And, being once resolved, set about the business, to all outward appearances, as calmly as if such incidents were the mere trivialities of his nightly life.

At a quarter after midnight he started to stroll from Charing Cross. At the half hour he was sauntering in the Westminster Abbey Gardens. He glanced along Victoria Street as far as he could see. An occasional omnibus came rumbling along. Cabs flitted to and fro; sometimes carriages.

But foot passengers were few and far between. And, so far as could be seen from the street, the buildings on either side of the way were in darkness.

He strolled gently on, swinging his stick, smoking a cigar, as any other gentleman might have done who enjoyed the cool night air. Under a lamp-post stood a policeman. Mr Holland smiled.

'Good-night, officer!'

He bestowed on him a genial salutation, which the other returned in kind.

'Good-night, sir.'

He seemed rather a youngish man, well set up, with broad shoulders and a shrewd face. Mr Holland wondered if he should, have any professional intercourse with him before the night was over. He laughed to himself as he thought of it. When he had gone some distance further he stopped and turned. The constable had vanished. Presumably his duty had led him down one of the side streets. An omnibus was coming in one direction, a couple of cabs in the other. Miss Bewicke's rooms were close at hand. Should he let the vehicles pass before he came to business? It was not yet one. He hesitated, then walked slowly past the house, noticing as he went that the front door was closed. What did it mean? Was he supposed to knock, calling upon the porter to let him in? The notion was absurd. Perhaps Miss Casata had only been playing with him after all.

At the idea he laughed again. What would Miss Broad say—and think—if the woman had promised more than she could perform? He went nearly as far as Victoria, then retraced his steps. As he approached the house again Big Ben struck one; He stopped, threw away the butt of his cigar, moved to the door. There was a handle. He turned it, it yielded, the door was open.

So it seemed that there was some sort of method in Miss Casata's madness.

The question was, Where was the porter? Was he within? Upstairs or down? He peeped inside the door, or tried to. The street lamps did not penetrate; it was pitch dark. He entered, closing the door behind him. All was still. As he listened, seeking to peer this way and that, it seemed to him that the darkness was like a wall on every side.

'What am I to do? I shall tumble over something if I don't look out; I don't even know where the staircase is: Dare I strike a match? I wonder what professionals do under circumstances such as these. I've heard of their carrying dark lanterns, and such-like mysterious things. Unfortunately, I haven't got so far as that, though there's no knowing how far I shall get before I've done.'

He moved forward, and kicked against something which made a noise.

'This will never do. I shall come to grief if I don't look out. It'll have to be a match.'

He struck one; it ignited with a spluttering noise which seemed to him to resemble the explosion of a dynamite cartridge, fizzled, then went out.

'This is pretty. But I caught a glimpse of the staircase. I suppose I'll have to be content with seeing so much.'

He felt his way to the stairs, presently had his hand upon the rail, then commenced to ascend. All at once he stopped.

'Hanged if I haven't forgotten on which floor her rooms are! That's a comfortable state of affairs. I can't go prowling all over the place playing a game of hide-and-seek with Miss Bewicke's rooms. There'd be trouble. Now, what am I to do?'

The question was answered in rather a curious way. Looking up he gradually became conscious of what looked like a gleam of light somewhere overhead.

'I wonder if that's a hint to me, or if it's the porter. I'm off to inquire. If it's the porter I'll have to explain.'

He chuckled to himself at the reflection of the sort of explanation he would have to offer. He continued to ascend.

'I hope it's all right, but it seems a good way up. I didn't think she occupied quite such an elevated position as this.'

He reached the floor on which was the light, perceiving now that it proceeded from a door upon the right which was open but the merest fraction of an inch.

'Is that where she resides? I wonder. At least I'll make inquiries. I'll knock, as an honest man should do, and see who answers.'

He tapped at the panel softly with his knuckles, so softly that one might have been excused for supposing he had no desire that his tapping should be heard. There was no response. He tapped again; still none. He pushed the door wider open, finding himself in what appeared, in the dim light, to be a little hall. Another open door was on his right. It was on the other side of this that the light was burning. He remembered what Miss Casata had said about Miss Bewicke's bedroom; that it was the second door on his right as he entered. Apparently she had been as good as her word; better, indeed, for she had placed a light to guide him. He advanced to find himself in what was evidently a lady's bedroom.

A night light flickered on a table in the centre; it was that which had lightened his darkness. He glanced around. Everywhere were traces of feminine occupation; knick-knacks which no man would willingly suffer in the chamber in which he slept; numerous examples of the inevitable photograph. Against a wall hung a crayon portrait. He recognised the original—the owner of the room. The pictured face seemed to return him look for look, reproaches in its glances. He removed his eyes, abashed.

On one side was the dressing-table of which Miss Casata had spoken. A gorgeous piece of furniture, of some delicate light wood, with gilt and ivory insets. Columns of drawers were on either side; a full-length cheval glass swung between them. As he stood in front of it he was startled by the reflection of his own image; he felt that there was something sinister in the bearing of the man who spied on him. The little drawers were those of which he had been told. They contained many of Miss Bewicke's jewels. What he sought was in the bottom drawer upon his right. Somehow, since he had entered the house, everything seemed on his right. He stooped to open it. The drawer was locked.

The discovery staggered him more than anything which had gone before—that the drawer was locked. At last he was confronted with the real nature of the errand he had come upon. Hitherto he had been able to salve his conscience with the fact that he had simply passed through open doors. Now, if he wished to effect an entrance he would have to force one, like any other thief. He gave another try at the handle. The drawer refused to budge. It certainly was locked. His eye was caught by something which was lying upon the floor, within a foot of him. It was a screwdriver. The juxtaposition was suggestive; the screwdriver, and the locked drawer. Miss Casata was no half-hearted ally; she was thorough. She was aware that, as an amateur, he might forget to bring the proper tools; so, with praiseworthy thoughtfulness, she had supplied, in advance, his possible omissions.

He was not so grateful as he might have been. He used strong language.

'Curse that woman! It is such as she who drive men along the road to hell.'

None the less he took the screwdriver in his hand. He felt its edge. It seemed sharp.

'I suppose, since I've gone so far, I may as well see the thing right through. It's no good shying at a gnat after tackling a whale. Here goes!'

Thrusting the chisel between the woodwork and the drawer, he proceeded to prise it open. The lock was but a slight one. It quickly yielded. The drawer shot out. He peered within. It contained a small white box, apparently of deal. He took it out. Inside was a ruby signet ring. He rose with the ring between his fingers.

As he stood up, someone came into the room. Turning, he found himself staring at Miss Bewicke.

CHAPTER VIII.
THE LADY—AND THE GENTLEMAN

Apparently each of the pair was equally surprised. Each stared at the other as if tongue-tied; Mr Holland motionless, holding the ring a little in front of him, as if suffering from at least temporary paralysis; Miss Bewicke, equally rigid, with her fingers up to her throat, just as she had raised them intending to remove the boa which was about her neck. It was she who first regained the faculty of speech.

'Guy!' The word came with a little gasp, as if she uttered it unwittingly. He was still; staring at her as if he were powerless to remove his eyes from off her face. 'What are you doing?'

Still silence from the man. His incapacity seemed to inspire her with confidence. She removed her boa, smiling as she did so. She sauntered here and there, eyeing things. She walked right round him, peering at him as she went. He might have been some mechanical figure, he endured so stolidly her ostentatious curiosity. Only he followed her with his glance as she passed round.

She did not speak when she had finished her inspection; with apparent indifference to his presence she took off her hat and coat. Unable, perhaps, to endure the situation any longer he struggled to obtain possession of his voice. It sounded harsh and husky.

'I thought you had gone to Brighton?'

'So you keep an observation on my movements, I see?' The words were accompanied by a smile which made him clench his fists so tightly that he drove the nails into the palms. She was folding up a veil, with a dainty show of peculiar care. 'I ought to be at Brighton; but I'm not. I meant to go; but I didn't. It was so late that I put off my journey till tomorrow; so I went to see some people instead. It was painfully slow; this promises to be better.'

Her airy manner, which seemed to him to be so pregnant with contempt, tried him more than reproaches might have done, or rage. He was so conscious of his position that indifference stung more than lashes. A policeman he could have faced, but not this smiling girl. All his self-respect had gone clean out of him; he felt she knew, and floundered in his efforts to regain some part of it.

'Miss Bewicke, you know why I am here.'

'To see me, I suppose. So good of you, Guy. Especially as I take it that you intended to wait for me till I returned from Brighton.'

'I came to take my own.'

'Your own?'

'This.'

He held out the ring between his finger and thumb. She came nearer, so that she might see what it was he held, smiling all the time.

'That—that's mine!'

'It was bequeathed me by my uncle.'

'Your uncle? Impossible; it wasn't his to bequeath.'

'You know the conditions which were attached to its possession. Since you declined to give it me—'

'I did not decline.'

'I don't know what other construction you put upon your conduct of last night. I gathered that you declined. Therefore, since its immediate possession was of capital importance, I came and took it.'

'How nice of you. And you waited till you thought I was at Brighton to show your mettle? How discreet! Guy, weren't you once to have been my husband?'

Nothing was further from his desire than to become involved in a tangle of reminiscences, so he became a little brutal.

'I have the ruby; that is the main point.'

'Are you proud of having robbed me—the girl who was to have been your wife?'

'You would have robbed me.'

'Even supposing that to be true, does that entitle you to throw aside all those canons of honour to which you have always given me to understand you were such a stickler, and become—a thief? Oh, Guy!'

'I do not propose to bandy words with you. I know of old your capacity to make black seem white—you were ever an actress, May. How the ruby originally came into your possession I cannot say.'

'It's not a pretty story, Guy; scarcely to your uncle's credit.'

'But you were perfectly well aware that morally it was mine. It was nothing to you; it was all the world to me. I believe that you refused to let me have it precisely because you knew that your refusal might entail my ruin; and so your cup of revenge might be filled to the full. Under those circumstances I hold that I was justified in using any and every means to save myself from being utterly undone by the whim of a revengeful woman.'

'I meant to let you have it.'

'That was not the impression you left upon my mind last night.'

'You took me unawares—I had to think things over.'

'Then if it was your intention that I should have it you cannot but be pleased to find that my action has kept abreast of your intention.'

Miss Bewicke was silent. She was drawing imaginary pictures with her finger-tip on the table by which she was standing, looking down as she did so. His desire was to get away; it was not an interview which he wished to have prolonged. But his departure was postponed.

'Why do you say I am revengeful?'

'You know better than I.'

'Do you think I wish to be revenged on you because once you pretended to love me, and now you keep up that pretence no longer?'

'It was no pretence.'

'I am glad to hear that, because, Guy, I love you still.'

She looked up at him in such a way that she seemed to compel him to meet her eyes. He shivered.

'I wish you wouldn't say such things.'

'Why? Because they're true? I like to tell the truth. I have always loved you, and I always shall, though I shall never be your wife.'

'I thought you said you were engaged to Dumville.'

'So I am. And I daresay that perhaps one day I shall marry him. I don't know quite why. But it certainly isn't because I love him. I have never pretended to. Ask him; he's frankness itself; he'll confess. Although, as you have only told me, I am a woman with ill-regulated passions and irresponsible tendencies, I'm a woman with only one love in her life, and you are he. Good-night, and good-bye.'

Now that she had formally dismissed him he felt that it was difficult to go. He fidgeted instead.

'I know you think that I have behaved meanly.'

'Not at all. I suppose you have acted according to your lights.'

'I'm not so sure of that. But, the truth is, I was desperate.'

'Indeed? Is that so? Like the man with the twelve starving children, who steals the bottle of whisky. I know. If I were you I wouldn't trouble to explain. This sort of situation is not improved by explanation. I think you had better pocket your booty and go.'

'As for the ruby'—he was holding it out on the palm of his open hand—'I will give you another for it a dozen times as good as this.'

For the first time she fired up.

'You dare to do anything of the kind—you dare! Do you think I am to be bought and sold?'

'I simply don't wish you to suffer from my action.'

'Do you think that your giving me one piece of stone in exchange for another piece of stone will prevent my suffering? Guy, please, go.'

He placed the ring before her on the table.

'There is the ruby.'

'Take it.'

'Do you mean that?'

'I do. If it is of the slightest use to you, by all means take it.'

'You give it to me—freely?'

'Oh, yes, so freely! Only—I wish you'd go.'

Thrusting the ruby into his waistcoat pocket, he went, without another word. Without it seemed darker even than before. He stumbled, blindly, down the stairs. Presently the darkness lightened; a gleam descended from above. Glancing up he perceived that Miss Bewicke was leaning over the railing with a lighted candle in her hand. He said nothing; attempted no word of thanks. So far as he knew she, too, was still; but as he descended, assisted by the light she held, he felt as he was convinced the whipped cur must feel, which sneaks off with its tail between its legs. The candle was still showing a faint glimmer of light as he passed into the street. He applied a dozen injurious epithets to himself as he thought that he had not even acknowledged the courtesy he had received. But for the life of him he could not, at that moment, have uttered a word of thanks.

Now that he was out in the street he raged. In his first mad impulse he would have taken what Miss Bewicke had called his 'booty' from his pocket and hurled it from him through the night. Prudence, however, prevailed. He told himself, again and again, that he was an ineffable thing to allow it to remain a second longer in his possession. It stayed there all the same. He was conscious that nothing could be less romantic than the whole adventure; nothing more undignified than the part which he had played in it. He had been throughout a mere figurehead—a counter manipulated by three women—he who thought that if he had anything on which to pride himself it was his manhood. His rage waxed hotter as he strode along; he was angry even with Miss Broad.

'If it hadn't been for her—' he began. Then stopped, stood still, struck with his fist at the air—his stick, it seemed, he had left behind him. 'What a cur I am! I try to put the blame, like some snivelling sneak of a schoolboy, upon everyone except myself, as though the fault was not mine, and mine alone. Am I some weak idiot that I am not responsible for my own actions? that I do a dirty thing, and then exclaim that someone made me? Well, it's done, and can't be undone, and I stand, self-confessed, a hound; but, as I live, I'll return at once and make her take the ruby back again. Then off once more for Africa. Better to be haunted by my uncle's ghost than by my own conscience.'

He turned, prepared to put his new-born resolution immediately into effect, and found himself confronted by an individual by whom his steps had been dogged ever since he left Miss Bewicke's. Had he had his wits about him he could hardly have helped noticing the fact, the proceedings of the person who took such a warm interest in his movements had been so singular. To begin with, he had been on the other side of the road. When Mr Holland first appeared he had slunk back into a doorway, from which he presently issued in pursuit, keeping as much as possible in the shadow.

When, however, he perceived himself unnoticed he became bolder. Until, at last, making a sudden dash across the street, he began to follow within a few feet of the unconscious pedestrian. He carried something, which every now and then he gripped with both hands, as if about to strike.

The mathematical moment came when Mr Holland turned. Without giving him a chance to speak the man swung the something which he carried through the air, bringing it down heavily, with a thud, upon his head. Mr Holland dropped on to the pavement. And there he lay.

CHAPTER IX.
THE FLYMAN

The assailant remained, for a second or two, looking down on his recumbent victim. He retained his grip upon his weapon, as if anticipating the possibility of having to strike with it another blow. But, no, the first had done its work. Mr Holland lay quite still, in an ugly heap, as men only lie who have been stricken hard. His assailant touched him with his foot, as if to make quite sure. Mr Holland did not resent the intrusion of the other's boot; he evinced no interest in it at all. The man was satisfied.

'That done him.'

It had, for sure. The fellow glanced up and down the street. No one was in sight. That was a state of things which could hardly be expected to continue. Time was precious; at any moment a policeman might appear. Under certain circumstances a policeman is inquisitive. The man, dropping on one knee, began to handle Mr Holland as if he had been so much dead meat; indeed, a butcher might have been expected to finger the carcase of what he had just now killed with greater ceremony.

'I wonder where he put it.'

He appeared to be searching for something, which, at first, he could not find. He went quickly through the stricken man's pockets, emptying each in turn of its contents. He made no bones about putting back what he took out, but threw everything into an inner pocket in his own jacket. Watch, money, cigar-case, keys, various odds and ends all went into the same receptacle. Still he did not appear to light on what he sought.

'Suppose he never got it? That would be a pretty little game. My crikey!'

He went through the pockets a second time more methodically; coat, waistcoat, trousers, nothing was omitted. The result was disappointing; they all were empty.

'Has he got it in a secret pocket?' Tearing open the waistcoat, he ran his fingers up and down the lining. 'I can't undress the bloke out here.' He went carefully over the lining, fingered the trousers. 'I don't believe he's got it. If he hasn't, then I'm done. It wasn't worth bashing him for this little lot.' The reference was, possibly, to what he had transferred to his own jacket. 'If he hasn't got it, there'll be trouble. Strikes me I'd better take a little trip into the country. He might think I'd got it and done a bunk. I might get a bit out of him like that. If he's anything to get. I wish I'd never gone in for the job. What's that?'

All the while he had never ceased to finger the silent man, submitting his garments to the minutest possible examination which the position permitted. Constantly he glanced behind and in front, well knowing that the risk of intrusion grew greater with every moment. With what looked very like impertinence, he turned the object of his curiosity over on to his face. As he did so his eye was caught by something which was lying on the pavement, and which apparently had hitherto been covered by the body of the silent man. It was a ring. He snatched at it.

'Got it, by the living jingo! The whole time the fool was right on top of it. If I hadn't overed him I might have gone away and thought he'd never had it after all. That'd been a pretty how-d'ye-do. I suppose he dropped it when I downed him, and covered it when he fell. He might have done it on purpose, just to spite me.' He was standing up, turning the ring over and over between his fingers. 'It's all right, there's no mistake about that much. This is fair jam, this is. A thousand quids into my pocket.' Something attracted his attention. 'Hollo!—sounded like a footstep—a copper's, unless I'm wrong!'

Without pausing to look behind he crossed the street, keeping well within the shadow of the houses, and walking fast, yet not too quickly, in the direction of Victoria. As he went he disposed of what had proved so efficient a weapon. It was a narrow bag, about a couple of inches in diameter, and a little over a foot in length. It was stuffed with sand. Untying one end, he allowed the contents to dribble out into the areas of the houses as he passed. Nothing remained but a strip of canvas. He was cramming this into his pocket as he reached the corner of a street into which he turned. A constable was standing on the kerb as if waiting for him to come. His wholly unexpected appearance might have startled a less skilful practitioner into doing something rash. But this gentleman had had too many curious experiences to permit himself to readily lose his wits.

'Good-night, p'liceman. Fine night!' he sang out, moving quickly on, as if he were hastening on.

'Good-night,' returned the policeman.

He eyed the other as he passed, as if he wondered who he was, yet was conscious of no legitimate reason why he should stop him to inquire.

The man drew in the morning air between his teeth, as if he desired to inflate his lungs to the full.

'That was a squeak. It wasn't him I nosed. Who'd have thought that he was there. If he'd come round the corner a minute or two ago there'd have probably been fun. Lucky I emptied the bag before I came on him. Hollo! He's going into Victoria Street. If he uses his eyes he'll spot my bloke in half a minute from now. I'd better put the steam on.'

He quickened his pace, not breaking into a run, for he was aware that nothing arouses attention more than the sight of a man running at that hour in a London street. But for the next ten minutes he moved at a good five miles an hour, going fair toe-and-heel. Then he slackened, judging that for the present he was safe; and, moreover, he was blown.

By what at least seemed devious ways he steered for Chelsea, to find himself, at last, in the King's Road. Thence he made for the river side, pausing before a house which faced the Thames. The house was an old one. In front was a piece of ground which was half yard, half garden. The approach to this was guarded by an iron railing and a gate. The gate was locked. By it was a rusty bell handle. At this he tugged. Almost immediately a window on the first floor was opened about three inches. A voice was heard.

'Who's there?'

'It's me, the Flyman.'

'You've been a devil of a time.'

'Couldn't be no quicker.'

The window was shut again. Presently the front door was opened instead. A man came out. It was Horace Burton. He sauntered to the gate.

'Have you got it?'

'You let me in and then I'll tell you.'

'Don't be an idiot! Tell me, have you got it?'

'I sha'n't tell you nothing till I'm inside.'

'You're an ass! Do you think I want to keep you out?' He fumbled with the lock. 'Confound this key; it's rusty.'

'Your hand ain't steady; that's what's wrong with it.'

'Hang the thing!'

The key dropped with a clatter to the ground.

'You let me have a try at it; perhaps my hand ain't so shaky as yours.'

The man outside picked up the fallen key, thrusting his hand through the railings to enable him to do so. Soon the gate was open. When he had entered he locked it again behind him. The two men went into the house. When they were in the hall Mr Burton repeated his assertion.

'You've been a devil of a time. Do you think I want to stop up all night waiting for you?'

'That's all right. I'll tell you all about it when we get upstairs. Who's there?'

'Old Cox is there, that's who's there; and he looks to me as if he were going to stop there the rest of his life—hanged if he doesn't.'

Possibly Mr Burton had been quenching his thirst too frequently with the idea of speeding the heavy hours of his vigil. The result was obvious in his speech and his appearance. At the foot of the staircase he stumbled against the bottom stair. The newcomer proffered his assistance.

'Steady, governor. Let me lend you a hand.'

Mr Burton was at once upon his dignity.

'Don't you touch me. I don't want your hand. Do you think I don't know my way up my own staircase?'

He ascended it as if in doubt. The Flyman kept close behind in case of accident. Which fact Mr Burton, when he was half way up, discovered. Steadying himself against the banister he addressed his too-assiduous attendant.

'Might I ask you not to tread upon my heels? Might I also ask you to go down to the bottom of the stairs and wait there till I'm at the top? There's too much of it.'

'All right, governor. Only don't keep me here too long, that's all.'

'You haven't kept me long? Oh, no! Not more than thirteen hours.'

When he had reached the top Mr Burton threw open the door of a room in which the gas was lighted. In an arm-chair a gentleman was smoking a cigar.

'This confounded Flyman thinks that he's the devil knows who. Seems to think he owns the place. I think I'll have a drink.'

The gentleman in the arm-chair ventured on remonstrance.

'I wouldn't if I were you; at least, not till we've got this business over.'

'Wouldn't you? Then I would. There's something the matter with this beastly siphon.'

The matter was that while he directed the nozzle of the siphon in one direction he held his glass in another. The result was that the liquor did not go where he intended. So he drank his whisky neat.

While Mr Burton was having his little discussion with the siphon, the man who had described himself as 'the Flyman' came into the room. He was rather over the average height, slightly built, with fair hair and moustache and very pale blue eyes. The eyes were his most peculiar feature. He was not bad looking, with an agreeable personality; at first sight, a likeable man, until you caught his eyes, then you wondered. They were set oddly in his head, so that they seldom seemed to move. He had a trick of regarding you with a curiously immobile stare, which, even when he smiled—which was but rarely—seemed to convey a latent threat. He was dressed like a respectable artisan, and had such a low-pitched, clear, musical voice that it was with surprise one observed how peculiar were his notions of his mother tongue.

As soon as he was inside the room Mr Burton repeated his former inquiry.

'Now, then, have you got it?'

'I have.'

'Then hand it over.'

Mr Burton held out a tremulous hand.

'Half a mo. I've got a word or two to say before we come to that. I should like you to understand how I did get it. It wasn't for the asking, I'd have you know.'

The gentleman in the arm-chair interposed. He waved his cigar.

'One moment.'

'Two, if you like, Mr Cox.'

He was a little, paunchy man, with 'Jew' written so large all over him that one asked oneself why he had been so ungrateful to his forefathers as to associate himself with such a name as Cox—Thomas Cox. He got out of his chair, which was much too large for him, so that he could see the Flyman, who still kept himself modestly in the background. He punctuated his words by making little dabs in the air with his cigar.

'What we want is the ruby; that's all we want. We don't want the schedule of your adventures. We're not interested. You understand?'

'Yes, I understand you, Mr Cox, but it don't go.'

'What do you mean, "it don't go"?'

'I'm not all alone in this. There's three of us in this game.'

'Listen to me. You say you've got the ruby. Very well, hand it over. I will see you have what Mr Burton promised you. We'll say no more about it, and there'll be an end of the matter.'

The Flyman's manner became a trifle dogged.

'I don't hand over nothing till you've heard what I've got to say.'

Something in the speaker's manner struck the observant Mr Cox. He showed signs of perturbation.

'Flyman, you haven't killed him?'

'I don't know whether I have or haven't. I hit, perhaps, a bit harder than I meant. He was as good as dead when I saw him last; anyhow, he'll be silly for the rest of his days, or else I'm wrong. I know what a good downer with a sand bag means. I'm a bit afraid I gave him an extra good one. I didn't like the looks of him at all.'

'You're a fool! Why did you do it?'

'Because you told me?'

'I told you! What the devil do you mean?'

'You set me on the job—you and Mr Burton together. You said to me there's a bloke coming out of a certain house at a certain time. He's got something on him which you're to get. You knew very well I wasn't going to get it out of him by asking.'

'Did anyone see you?'

'Not while I was at it, so far as I know. But a copper did directly afterwards. For all I can tell, he's seen me before, and'll know me again.'

Mr Cox's perturbation visibly increased.

'Did he—did he try to arrest you?'

'He didn't know what had happened then; but he was going straight to where I'd left the bloke lying. Then, of course, he'd put two and two together, and think of me.'

'Flyman, you're a fool! Did anybody see you come in here?'

'That's more than I can say. But somebody'll soon know I did come in here if anything happens to me. I'm not going to be on this lay all on my own.'

Mr Cox threw his unfinished cigar into the fireplace. It had gone out. His attention was occupied by matters which rendered smoking difficult. He stood knawing the finger-nails of his left hand. The Flyman watched him. Mr Burton seemed to be endeavouring to obtain sufficient control of his faculties to understand what the conversation was about. Presently Mr Cox delivered himself of the result of his cogitation.

'I tell you what, I shouldn't be surprised if a little trip abroad would do you good.'

'I'm willing.'

'Then I'll see that you have a berth on board a boat I know of, which leaves the London docks to-morrow for America.'

'I'm game.'

'Now, let's have the ruby.'

'Against the quids?'

'Against the quids. You don't suppose that Mr Burton and I carry a thousand pounds about with us loose in our pockets?'

'No quids, no ruby.'

'The money shall be handed to you when you're on board the ship.'

'I'll see that the ruby isn't handed to you till it is.'

'Do you think I want to do you?'

'I'm dead sure you do, if you only get a chance. I've done a little business with you before to-day, Mr Cox. You must think I'm soft. Why, nothing would suit your book better than to do me out of the pieces and get me lagged. But if you try that game, I'll see you get a bit of it. Thank you; I don't trust you, not as far as I can see you, Mr Cox.'

The gentleman thus flatteringly alluded to laughed, a little mechanically.

'I'm sorry to hear you talk like that, Flyman. There's no time now to try to induce you to form a better opinion of me; but you'll discover that you have done me an injustice before very long. Anyhow, let's see that you have the ruby.'

Mr Burton chose this moment to awake to the fact that he had a very definite interest in the discussion which was being carried on. He banged his glass against the table.

'I'm going to have that ruby! I'm going to have it now!'

'So you shall, when you've given me the thousand pounds.'

'I don't care about the thousand pounds; I'm going to have the ruby!'

'Then, I'm damned if you are!'

'I say I am. Now, then! So you'd better give it to me—before I take it.'

The speaker staggered towards the Flyman.

'Don't you be silly, Mr Burton, or you might find me nasty; and I don't want to have to be nasty to you.'

'Give me the ruby; it's mine.'

'That's where you're wrong. Just now it happens to be mine.'

Mr Cox placed himself between the pair.

'Pretend to be sober, Burton, even if you're drunk.'

'I am sober. I don't care that for him.' He tried to snap his fingers, but the attempt was a disastrous failure. 'I say, I'm going to have the ruby now, and so I am.'

'Shut it!'

Mr Cox's treatment of the intoxicated gentleman was vigorous and to the point. He gave him a push which propelled him backwards with such unexpected force that, before he was able to recover himself, he was lying on the ground.

There for a time he stayed. The others paid no attention to him whatever. Mr Cox continued the discussion on his own account.

'Let me see the ruby.'

'Let me see the quids.'

'Look here, Flyman; you say you know me. Well, I know you; I know you for a windbag and a liar. It's quite likely that all you've been telling us is humbug, and that you've not been within miles of what we want. If you've got the ruby, you let me look at it; there'll be no harm done. I'm not going to buy a pig in a poke, and I'm not going to steal it.'

'I lay you are not going to steal it; I lay that. There it is. Now, you can take and look at it.'

Taking a ring from his waistcoat pocket, slipping it on to his little ringer, he held it out for the other's inspection, eyeing Mr Cox in a very singular manner as that gentleman bent over to examine it.

'Did you get that from—the person we've been talking about?'

'I did.'

'To-night?'

'To-night. Not an hour ago—as he came out of the house.'

Mr Cox turned to Mr Burton, who was sitting upon the floor.

'Get up, you jackass! Come here and see if this is what we're after.'

Mr Burton's answer was not exactly a response to this peremptory invitation.

'I'm not feeling—as I ought to feel.'

'So I should think. You'll soon be feeling still less as you ought to feel, if you don't look out.' He assisted the gentleman on to his feet. 'Now, then, pull yourself together. Come and see if what the Flyman's got is your uncle's ring.'

As Mr Burton advanced, the Flyman dropped the hand with the ringed finger.

'Don't you let him snatch at it, or I'll down him.'

'He won't snatch at it. You needn't be afraid of him.'

'I'm not afraid of him—hardly; only I thought I'd just give you a little warning, that's all. There you are, Mr Burton; there's what's worth more to you than you're likely to tell me.'

Mr Burton only bestowed upon the outstretched hand a momentary glance; he drew back as if what he saw had stung him.

'It's not!'

'What d'ye mean?'

'It's not my uncle's ring.' The fall, or something, had sobered him. He had become disagreeable instead. He snarled, showing his teeth to the gums, as if he would have liked to assail the man in front of him with tooth and nail. 'Curse you, Flyman! what's the game you're playing?'

'What's the game you think you're playing, that's what I want to know?'

'That's not my uncle's ring, and you know it's not. Come, out with it! no tricks here!'

'This is your uncle's ring, and you're trying to kid me that it isn't, thinking to do me out of what you promised. Don't you try that on, Mr Burton, or you'll be sorry.'

The two men glared at each other with their faces close together, Mr Burton meeting the Flyman's threatening glances without flinching. He turned to Mr Cox.

'Cox, what he's got on his finger is no more my uncle's ring than I am.'

'You're sure of that?'

'Dead certain. The stone in my uncle's ring was much larger, better colour, finer altogether. It bore his crest—on that thing there seems to be a monogram—and inside the gold mount, at the back, his name was engraved—"George Burton."'

'We can soon settle that part of the question. Flyman, is there a name inside that ring?'

The Flyman was already looking for himself.

'There's not; there's no name. Is this a plant between you two to do me out of my fair due?'

'Don't you make any mistake about that, my man. If that's the ring we want you shall have your thousand right enough. It's worth all that to us. If it's not, then it's worth nothing, and less than nothing. Don't let's have any error about this, Burton. You're quite sure that you recollect what your uncle's ring was like?'

'I'd pick it out among ten thousand. I've seen it hundreds—I should think, thousands—of times. I wore it myself for a year. It used to amuse the old man to fool about with it, lending it to all sorts of people. He lent it to me, and he lent it to Guy. I believe he lent it to Miss Bewicke; and it was because, when he asked her, she wouldn't give it him back again that he got his back up.'

'I suppose, Flyman, it was Mr Holland you tackled?'

'It was the bloke you pointed out to me this afternoon—that I do know. Here, I borrowed these things from off him—took them out of his pockets.' He produced a miscellaneous collection. Here's a cigar-case with initials on it, "G. H.," and cards inside with a name on them, "Mr Guy Holland." I should think that that ought to be about good enough.'

'You're sure that that was the only ring he had about him?'

'I'll swear to it. I ran the rule over him quite half a dozen times. He only had one ring—there wasn't one upon his hands—and that's it.'

'And you, Burton, are certain it's not your uncle's?'

'As sure as that I'm alive.'

'Then, in that case, we're done.'

The trio looked as if they were.

CHAPTER X.
SHE WISHES THAT SHE HADN'T

Miss Broad had a very bad night. That was because of her conscience, which pricked her. Almost as soon as Mr Holland had left her she regretted the advice she had given him—advice, she had the candour to admit, as applied to this case, being but a feeble word. She had bullied him into committing burglary! It was awful to think of, or, at least, it became awful by degrees. A sort of panorama of dreadful imaginings began to unfold itself in front of her. She even pictured him as being caught in the act, arrested, thrown into gaol, tried, sentenced to penal servitude, working in the quarries—she had heard of 'the quarries'—because of her. She did not pause to consider that, after all, he was responsible for his own actions. He loved her; by obedience he proved it, even to the extent of committing burglary. Therefore, the blame of what she did was on her shoulders.

So she upbraided herself, regretting too late, as ladies sometimes do, the line of action she had taken up with so much vigour.

'I wish I'd bitten my tongue off before I'd been so wicked. The truth is, I really believe I'd like to kill that woman. Ellen, you needn't pull my hair right out.'

The first two remarks were addressed to herself, the last, aloud, to her maid. That young person, who was dressing Miss Broad for dinner, found her mistress in rather a trying mood.

'If he was detected in the act, he would be at that woman's mercy. She might compel him to do anything in order to avoid open humiliation and disgrace and ruin.'

At the thought of what he might be compelled to do, she was divided between terror, tears and rage. Since the woman had once pretended to love him, and, no doubt, was still burning with a desire to be his wife, she might even force him—oh, horrible!

'Ellen, you're pulling my hair again.'

Which was not to be wondered at, considering how unexpectedly the young lady jerked her head.

She ate no dinner, excused herself from two engagements, made herself generally so agreeable that she drove her father to remark that her temper was not improving, and he pitied the man who had anything to do with her. Which observation added to her misery, for she knew quite well that her temper was her weakest point. She was a wretch, and she had ruined him!

Throughout the night she scarcely slept. She was continually getting off the bed to pace the room, exclaiming,—

'I wonder if he's doing it now?'

She must have wondered if he was doing it 'now' nearly a hundred times, apparently under the impression that 'it' was an operation which took time.

The result was that, when the morning came, she did not feel rested, and looked what she felt, causing her father—an uncomfortably observant gentleman, who prided himself, with justice, on being able to say as many disagreeable things as any man—to remark that she looked 'vinegary,' which soured Miss Broad still more.

She had an appointment with Mr Holland, at the usual place in Regent's Park, for ten. They were to have a little conversation; then, together, they were to go to church. She was at the rendezvous at nine, though how she managed to do it was a mystery even to herself. At ten minutes past she began to fidget, at the half-hour she was in a fever, and when ten o'clock struck, and there was no Mr Holland, she was as nearly beside herself as she could conveniently be.

'He's never been late before—never, never! Oh, what has happened?'

She went a little way along a path by which she thought that he might come; then, fearful that after all he might come another way, tremulously retracing her steps, she returned to the seat. But she could not sit still, nor stand still either. She was up and down, sitting and standing, fidgeting here and there, glancing in every direction, like the frightened creature she was rapidly becoming. Every nerve in her body was on edge. When the quarter struck, and there were no signs of Mr Holland, she could restrain herself no longer. Tears blinded her eyes; she had to use her handkerchief before she could see. It would have needed very little for her to become hysterical.

She knew her man—his almost uncanny habit of punctuality. She was certain that, if nothing serious had happened to prevent him, he would have been in time to a moment. She was sure, therefore, that something had happened. But what?

As she vainly asked herself this question, a boy came along one of the paths. He was a small child, about nine years of age, evidently attired in his Sunday best. He carried something in his hand. Coming up to her, he said,—

'Are you Miss Broad?' She nodded; she could not speak. 'I was told to give you this.'

He handed her the envelope. She jumped to the conclusion that it came from him. Her delight at receiving even a message from him about scattered her few remaining senses.

'I'll give you sixpence.' She spoke with a stammer, fumbling with her purse. 'I haven't one; I'll give you half-a-crown instead.'

The boy went off mumbling what might have been meant for thanks, probably too surprised at the magnitude of the gift to be able to make his meaning clear. She tore the envelope open. It contained half a sheet of paper, on which were the words,—

'If you want Mr Guy Holland, inquire of Miss May Bewicke.'

CHAPTER XI.
THE PURSUIT OF THE GENTLEMAN

That was all.

Miss Broad's first blundering impression was that somebody was having a joke with her—that she was mistaken, had read the words askew. She looked again.

No; the error, if error there were, was, to that extent, certainly not hers; the words were there as plain as plain could be, and they only.

'If you want Mr Guy Holland, inquire of Miss May Bewicke.'

They were typewritten, occupying a couple of lines. The rest of the sheet was blank—no address, no date, no signature; not a hint to show from whom the message could have come. She looked at the envelope. The face of it was blank; there was nothing on it, inside or out. Where was the boy who had brought it? She turned to see. He had gone, was out of sight. So far as she could perceive, she had the immediate neighbourhood entirely to herself. What did it mean?

The disappointment was so acute that, as she sank back upon the seat, the earth seemed to be whirling round in front of her. She never quite knew whether for a second or two she did not lose her senses altogether. When next she began to notice things, she perceived that the envelope had fallen to the ground, and that the half sheet of paper would probably have followed it had it not been detained by a fold in her dress. She examined them both again, this time more closely, without, however, any satisfactory result.

Of the typewritten words she could make neither head nor tail. Were they meant as a hint—a warning—what? Anyhow, from whom could they have come—to her, there, in the Park? Why had she not asked the boy who had instructed him to give the envelope to her? What a simpleton she had been!

'"Inquire of Miss May Bewicke." What can it mean? "Inquire of Miss May Bewicke." Unless—'

Unless it meant something she did not care to think of. She left the sentence unfinished, even in her own mind.

She arrived at a sudden resolution. It was too late for church, or she told herself it was, supposing her to have been in a church-going mood, which she most emphatically was not. Instead of church she would go to Mr Holland's rooms in Craven Street, and inquire for him there. Under the circumstances, anything, including loss of dignity—and she flattered herself that dignity, as a rule, was her strong point—was better than suspense.

She had some difficulty in finding a cab. In that district of town, cabs do not ply in numbers on Sunday morning. By the time she discovered one she was hot, dusty and, she feared, dishevelled. As the vehicle bore her towards the Strand, her sense of comfort did not increase. If he was not in Craven Street, what should she do? Ye saints and sinners! if he were in gaol!

He was not in Craven Street.

A matronly, pleasant-faced woman opened the door to her.

'Is Mr Holland in?'

'No, miss, he's not.'

'Has he been long gone out?'

'Well, miss, he hasn't been in all night.'

The young lady shivered. The landlady eyed her with shrewd, yet not unfriendly, eyes. She hazarded a question,—

'Excuse me, miss, but are you Miss Broad?'

'That is my name.'

'Would you mind just stepping inside?'

The landlady led the way into a front room. The first thing the young lady saw on entering was her photograph staring at her from the centre of the mantelshelf. A little extra colour tinged her cheeks. The landlady glanced from the original to the likeness, and back again.

'It's very like you, miss, if you'll excuse my saying so. You see, Mr Holland has told me all about it. You have my congratulations, if I might make so bold, for a nicer gentleman I never want to see. I was that pleased when I saw him come walking in the other day. Did you expect to see him, miss?'

'I had an appointment with him. He never kept it. As he has never done such a thing before, I scarcely knew what to think.'

'Well, miss, the truth is, I hardly know what I ought to say.'

'Say everything, please.'

'It was only his nonsense, no doubt, but when he was going out last night I asked him if he should be late. "Well, Mrs Pettifer," he said, "if I am late, you'd better make inquiries for me at Westminster Police Station, for that's where I shall be; they'll have locked me up." When Matilda told me this morning that he hadn't been in all night, I thought of his words directly, because he'd ordered his breakfast for eight o'clock this morning, and, as you say, he's always so dependable—Why, miss, whatever is the matter?'

Miss Broad, who had found refuge in an armchair, was looking very queer indeed.

'Don't you take on, miss. It was only his fun. Mr Holland's full of his jokes. Heaps of gentlemen stay out all night; nothing's happened.'

But the young lady was not to be comforted. She had her own reasons for being of a different opinion. That allusion to Westminster Police Station did not sound like a joke to her. When she quitted Craven Street, she directed the cabman to drive her to a certain number in Victoria Street. She was staring as she went at the two typewritten lines which the mysterious boy had brought in the mysterious envelope.

'I will inquire of Miss Bewicke. It will be better to begin there than—at the other place. There will be time enough for that afterwards. If—if she should have locked him up!'

The potentiality was too horrible. She could not bear to contemplate it. Yet, willy-nilly, it intruded on her fears.

She ascended in the lift to Miss Bewicke's apartments. She knocked with a trembling hand at Miss Bewicke's door. She had to knock a second time before an answer came. Then the door was opened by a tall, thin, saturnine-looking woman, to whom the visitor took a dislike upon the spot.

'Is Miss Bewicke at home?'

'Will you walk in?' It was only when Miss Broad had walked in that she learned that her quest was vain. 'Miss Bewicke is not at home. She went to Brighton this morning.'

'This morning? I thought she was going last night.'

'Who told you that?'

There was something in the speaker's voice which brought the blood to Miss Broad's cheeks with a rush. She stammered.

'I—I heard it somewhere.'

'Your information was learned on good authority; very good. Oh, yes, she meant to go last night, but she was prevented.'

'Prevented—by what?'

'I am not at liberty to say. Are you a friend of Miss Bewicke's?'

There was something in the woman's manner which Miss Broad suspected of being intentionally offensive. She stared at her with bold, insolent eyes, with, in them, what the young lady felt was the suggestion of an insolent grin. That she knew her, Miss Broad was persuaded; she was sure, too, that she was completely cognisant of the fact that she was not Miss Bewicke's friend.

'I am sorry to say that I am not so fortunate as to be able to number myself among Miss Bewicke's friends. I have not even the pleasure of her acquaintance.'

'That is unfortunate, as you say. About her friends Miss Bewicke is particular.'

The suggestion was so gratuitous that Miss Broad was startled.

'Are you a friend of hers?'

'I am her companion; but not for long. You know what it is for one woman to be a companion to another woman. It is not to be her friend. Oh, no. I have been a companion to Miss Bewicke for many years; but soon I go. I have had enough.'

The woman's manner was so odd that Miss Broad wondered if she was a little touched in the head, or if she had been drinking. She looked round the room, at a loss what to say. Her glance lighted on a large panel photograph which occupied the place of honour on the mantelpiece. It was Mr Holland. She recognised it with a start. It was the best likeness of him she had seen. He had not given her a copy, nor any portrait of himself, which was half as good.

Miss Bewicke's companion was watching her.

'You are looking at the photograph? It is Mr Holland, a friend of Miss Bewicke's, the dearest friend she has in the world.'

'You mean he was her friend?'

'He was? He is—none better. Miss Bewicke has many friends—oh, yes, a great many; she is so beautiful—is she not beautiful?—but there are none of them to her like Guy.'

The woman's familiar use of Mr Holland's Christian name stung Miss Broad into silence. That she lied she knew; to say that, to-day, Mr Holland was still Miss Bewicke's dearest friend was to attain the height of the ridiculous. That the young lady knew quite well. She was also aware that, for some reason which, as yet, she did not fathom, this foreign creature was making herself intentionally offensive. None the less, she did not like to hear her lover spoken of in such fashion by such lips. Still less did she like to see his portrait where it was. Had she acted on the impulse of the moment, she would have torn it into shreds. And perhaps she might have gone even as far as that had she not perceived something else, which she liked, if possible, still less than the position occupied by the gentleman's photograph.

On a table lay a walking-stick. A second's glance was sufficient to convince her of the ownership. It was his—a present from herself. She had had it fitted with a gold band; his initials, which she had had cut on it, stared her in the face. What was his walking-stick—her gift—doing there?

The woman's lynx-like eyes were following hers.

'You are looking at the walking-stick? It, also, is Mr Holland's.'

'What is it doing here?'

The woman shrugged her shoulders.

'He left it behind him, I suppose. Perhaps he was in too great a hurry, or Miss Bewicke. Sometimes, when one is in a great hurry to get away, one forgets little things which are of no importance.'

She called his walking-stick—her gift to him—a thing of no importance! What was the creature hinting at? Miss Broad would not condescend to ask, although she longed to know.

'As I tell you, Miss Bewicke is not at home. She is at the Hotel Metropole at Brighton. Would you like to take Mr Holland's walking-stick to—her?' There was an accent on the pronoun which the visitor did not fail to notice. 'What name shall I give to Miss Bewicke?'

'I am Miss Broad.'

'Miss Broad—Letty Broad? Oh, yes, I remember. They were talking and laughing about you—Mr Holland and she. Perhaps, after all, you had better not go down to Brighton.'

When the young lady was back in the street, her brain was a tumult of contradictions. That the woman who called herself Miss Bewicke's companion had, for reasons of her own, been trying to amuse herself at her expense she had not the slightest doubt. That Mr Holland's relations with Miss Bewicke were not what were suggested she was equally certain. None the less she wondered, and she doubted. What was his portrait doing there? Still more, what was his walking-stick? He was carrying it when they last met. Under what circumstances, between this and then, had it found its way to where it was? Where was Mr Holland? That there was a mystery she was convinced. She was almost convinced that Miss Bewicke held the key to it.

Should she run down to Brighton and find out? She would never rest until she knew. She had gone so far; she might as well go farther. She would be there and back in no time. The cabman was told to drive to Victoria. At Victoria a train was just on the point of starting. Miss Broad was travelling Brightonwards before she had quite made up her mind as to whether she really meant to go. When the train stopped at Clapham Junction, she half rose from her seat and all but left the carriage. She might still be able to return home in time for luncheon. But while she dilly-dallied, the train was off. The next stoppage was at Croydon. There would be nothing gained by her alighting there; so she reached Brighton, as she assured herself, without ever having had the slightest intention of doing it. Therefore, and as a matter of course, when the train rattled into the terminus she was not in the best of tempers. She addressed sundry inquiries to herself as she descended to the platform.

'Now what am I to do? I may as well go to the Metropole as I am here. I am not bound to see the woman even if I go. And as for speaking to her'—she curled her lip in a way which was intended to convey a volume of meaning—'I suppose it is possible to avoid the woman, even if I have the misfortune to be under the same roof with her. The hotel's a tolerable size; at anyrate, we'll see.'

She did see, and that quickly. As she entered the building, the first person she beheld coming towards her across the hall was Miss May Bewicke.

Which proves, if proof be necessary, that a building may be large, and yet too small.

CHAPTER XII.
THE TENDER MERCIES OF TWO LADIES

By way of a commencement, Miss Broad was conscious of two things—that Miss Bewicke was looking her best; that she herself was looking her worst; at least, she was nearly certain she was looking her worst, she felt so hideous.

Miss Bewicke had a knack of walking—it came by nature, though there were those who called it a trick—which gave her a curious, and, indeed, humorous, air of importance altogether beyond anything her stature seemed to warrant. This enabled her to overwhelm men, and even women who were much taller than herself, with a grace which was positively charming. She moved across that spacious hall, looking straight at Miss Broad, as if there was nothing there; and was walking past with an apparent unconsciousness of there being anyone within a mile, though she brushed against the other's skirts as she passed, which was a little more than Miss Broad could endure. She was not going all the way to Brighton to be treated by that woman as if she were a nonentity.

'Miss Bewicke!'

The lady, who had passed, turned.

'I beg your pardon?'

'Can I speak to you?'

'Speak to me?' She regarded the other with a smile which, if pretty, was impertinent. 'I'm afraid I haven't the pleasure.'

'I am Miss Broad.'

'Broad?—Broad? I don't seem to remember.'

'Perhaps you remember Mr Holland.'

'Mr Holland?—Guy Holland? Oh, yes, I have good cause for remembering him.'

'Mr Holland has spoken of me to you?'

'Oh! You are that Miss Broad! I have pleasure in wishing you good morning.'

Miss Bewicke walked off as if, so far as she was concerned, the matter was at an end; but so abrupt a termination to the interview the other would not permit.

'I am sorry to detain you, Miss Bewicke, but, as I have said, I wish to speak to you.'

'Yes. What do you wish to say?'

'Can I not speak to you in private?'

'By all means.' Miss Bewicke led the way into a sitting-room. As soon as they were in, and the door closed, before the other had a chance to open her lips, she herself began the ball. 'Miss Broad, before you speak, there is something which I wish to say to you. You incited Mr Guy Holland to commit, last night, a burglary upon my premises.'

If she expected the other to show signs of confusion, or to attempt denial, she was mistaken. Miss Broad did not flinch.

'I did.'

'You admit it?'

'I do.'

'Are you aware that in so doing you were guilty of a criminal action?'

'As to that I know nothing, and care less.'

'I have only to send for a policeman to have you sentenced to a term of imprisonment.'

'I understand how it is you have been so successful on the stage. You really are an excellent actress. You bear yourself as if you were the injured party, while all the time you know very well that it was precisely because you had robbed him that I advised him to despoil you of your booty.'

'You are perfectly aware that that is false.'

'On the contrary, I am perfectly aware that it is true. Where is Mr Holland? Is he here with you?'

'Miss Broad!'

'Or did you dare to make his doing, what you know he was perfectly justified in doing, an affair of the police?'

'I came upon Guy Holland, at dead of night, engaged in robbing me, and I sent him from me with my blessing.'

'Then where is he?'

'I know no more than this chair.'

'Miss Bewicke, I called at your rooms this morning. I saw his walking-stick upon your table. When I asked how it came there, the woman who had opened the door said, in effect, that he had left it behind in his hurry to go away with you.'

'The woman! What woman?'

'She said she was your companion.'

'Casata? Louise Casata never said anything so monstrous.'

'Not in so many words; but that was what she intended me to understand.'

'You believed it? What a high opinion you appear to have of us! Guy must be worse even than I imagined, or you, his promised wife, would not judge him with such hard judgment.'

'I did not believe it; but I did believe that you called in the police last night.'

'I didn't; I called in no one. I simply told him to go, and he went.'

'You are laughing. You know where he is. I can see it in your face.'

'Then you are indeed a seer.'

'This morning, when he did not come, as he promised he would, and always has done, someone gave me this. What am I to think?'

Miss Broad handed Miss Bewicke the two typewritten lines, which that lady carefully regarded.

'Someone? Who was someone?'

'A little boy. I thought it was a message from Guy. By the time I found it wasn't, he was gone. I don't know who he was, nor from whom he came, if it wasn't from you.'

It certainly did not come from me. Miss Broad, I begin to find you amusing. I also begin to understand what it is Guy Holland perceives in you to like. You are more of a woman than I am; that is, there is in you more of the natural savage, which, to a man of his temperament, goes to make a woman.'

'I want none of your praises.'

'I'm not going to give you any, or compliments either. I doubt if you're in a frame of mind to properly appreciate any sort of sleight-of-hand. Let me finish. I had an engagement for luncheon; as you have made me late for it, perhaps you will do me the honour of lunching with me here.'

'No, thank you.'

'Pardon me, you will.'

'Excuse me, I won't.'

'We shall see.'

Miss Bewicke touched the bell button. Miss Broad eyed her with flaming cheeks.

'It's no use your ordering anything to eat for me, because I sha'n't touch it. You treat me as if I were a child. I'm not a child.'

'My dear Miss Broad, we are both of us women—both of us; and there are senses in which women and children are synonyms. Mr Holland was once in love with me—he was, I assure you. He is now in love with you, which fact creates between us a bond of sympathy.'

'I don't see it.'

'No? I do. You will. He appears to have got himself into, we will put it, a rather equivocal position. It is our bounden duty, as joint sympathisers, to get him out of it. We will discuss our bounden duty; but I never can discuss anything when I'm starving, which I am.'

To the waiter who appeared Miss Bewicke gave orders for an immediate lunch for two. Miss Broad kept silence. The truth was, she was not finding Miss Bewicke altogether the sort of person she expected. That little lady went on,—

'I'm free to confess, my dear Miss Broad; by the way, may I call you Letty?'

'No; you may not.'

'Thank you; you are so sweet. As I was about to remark, my dear—Letty'—the other winced, but was still—'I'm free to confess that I think it not improbable that something has happened to Mr Holland.'

'You know that something has happened?'

116

'I don't know—I surmise. I put two and two together, thus:—To begin with, I don't think that you were the only person who egged him on to felony.'

Miss Broad again was speechless. She remembered Mr Holland's tale of his encounter with Miss Casata.

'There was a preciseness about his proceedings which set me thinking at the time, and has kept me thinking ever since. I'm pretty shrewd, you know. Now, I happen to be aware that a certain person of my acquaintance has been on too good terms with Mr Horace Burton. You have heard of Mr Horace Burton? I thought so. Such a nice young man! Now, however, this certain person is on the worst terms with Mr Horace Burton. For sufficient reasons, I assure you. She has been evolving fantastic schemes of vengeance on the deceitful wretch; she's just a little cracked, you know. To ruin Mr Horace Burton by assisting Guy Holland to deprive him of his fortune would be just the kind of notion which would commend itself to her. I fancy that that's exactly what she did do. Didn't she, my dear?'

Miss Broad was breathing a little hard. The other's keen intuition startled her.

'It was I who told him to take what was his own.'

'Yes, I know; but the first suggestion did not come from you. However, so long as we understand each other, that's the point. To proceed—Mr Horace Burton would be cautious that this certain person's sweetness had turned to gall, and also that she was wishful to pay him out in his own coin. He might even have a notion of the form that payment was to take, having learned it from the certain person's own lips. If so, you may be quite sure that he or his friends saw Guy Holland enter my premises, if nobody else did. They saw him come out. They were to the full as anxious to obtain possession of that ruby as ever he could be. So they took it from him.'

'Took it from him—with violence?'

'Do you think they could take it from him without violence—that he would hand it over practically upon request? That's not like Guy; not the Guy I knew. He'd fight for it tooth and nail himself against a regiment.'

'Do you think then they hurt him?'

'It looks as if they did something to him. He never went home. There must have been some reason why he didn't. There is at least a possibility that it was because he couldn't.'

'Do you think they—killed him?'

'Ah, now you ask too much. I should say certainly not. It would be unintentionally if they did. That would be too big a price even for Mr Horace Burton to pay. If they attacked him in fair fight, I should say that he killed someone before they did him; and that when they did it was because they had to. But the possibility is that they never let him have a chance; that they stole on him unawares, and had him at their mercy before he knew that danger threatened.'

'Miss Bewicke, you are so clever—so much cleverer than I—'

'My dear!'

'Come up to town with me and help me look for him, and go with me to the police, and—'

'Set all London by the ears? I know. We'll do it; but here comes lunch. You sit down to lunch with me, and we'll talk things over while we lunch. You see how far talking things over has already brought us; and after lunch we'll go to town, as you suggest, and find out what's happened to Guy Holland, and where he is, or we'll know the reason why. But if you won't lunch with me, then nothing remains but to wish you good day, and, so far as I'm concerned, there'll be an end of the matter. I'll have nothing to do with a person who won't eat my bread and salt.'

So the ladies lunched together. Although Miss Broad declared that she could not swallow a morsel, Miss Bewicke induced her to dispose of several. Indeed, she handled her with so much skill that by the time the meal was through— it was not a long one—one would have thought that they really were on decent terms with one another, though Miss Broad was still a trifle scratchy. But then her nerves were out of order, and when a lady's nerves are out of order, she is apt, occasionally, to stray from those well-defined paths which etiquette and good breeding require her to tread; in short, she does not know what she is doing, or what anybody else is doing either, which Miss Bewicke quite understood, so that her guest's eccentricities, apparently, simply amused her.

And the two young ladies went up together in the same compartment to London to look for Mr Holland, and to call down, if necessary, vengeance on his enemies and those who had despitefully used him.

CHAPTER XIII.
VISITORS FOR MISS CASATA

Miss Casata had a razor in her hand—an open razor. She examined its edge.

'It is very sharp. Oh, yes, how sharp! One cut; it will all be over. Will it be over with one cut—that is it—or shall I have to hack, and hack, and hack? That would not be agreeable.'

She stood in front of a looking-glass, regarding her own reflection.

'I am not bad looking; no, I am not. I have a certain attractiveness, which is my own. To use the razor would be to make a mess. I should be a horrible sight. Would he care? He would not see me. If he did, he would laugh, I know. He has what he calls a taste for the horrible. It would amuse him to behold me all covered with blood.'

She turned her attention to some articles which were on a table.

'Here is a revolver. The six barrels are all loaded. It would not need them all to blow out my brains—that is, if I have any to blow. Here is a bottle of hydrocyanic acid. What lies I had to tell to get it; what tricks I had to play! There is enough in this little bottle to kill the whole street. I have, therefore, the keys of death close to my hand—painless, instant death. Three roads to eternal sleep, and I stand so much in need of rest. Yet I hesitate to use them. It is very funny. Is it because I am going mad—I did not use to be infirm of purpose—I wonder?'

She handled, one after another, the three objects—the razor, the revolver, the little bottle—as if endeavouring to make a selection.

'I am too optimistic. There is my fault—I always hope. It is an error. I have always had in my life such evil fortune that, when happiness came, I should have known it would not endure—that the night would be blacker because the sun once shone; that for me, henceforward, it would be always night. I was a fool; so happy I forgot, so I pay for it. Well, I will take my fate into my own hands and make an ending when I choose. I should have liked to see the little one—my little one.' A softness came into the voice of which one might hardly have thought it capable. 'To have held it in my arms; to press it to my breast; to touch its lips with mine. I should, indeed, have liked to be a mother. Yet better not; it might have been like its father. That would have been the worst of all. Which is it to be—steel? lead? a little drink? Why is it I cannot decide? What's that?'

She had Miss Bewicke's dainty drawing-room to herself. An incongruous object she seemed in it, she and her gruesome playthings. A sound appeared to have caught her ear. She put her right hand behind her back; in it, the three assistants of death. Moving to a door which was on the opposite side of the room, turning the handle softly, she passed half-way through it, then stood and listened.

'Quite still, yet. The noise did not come from there. There was a noise. Ah!'

The interjection was in response to a rat-tat-tat on the knocker. The room was illuminated by a dozen electric lights. Disconnecting one after the other, she allowed but a single one to remain alight. Comparatively, the apartment was in darkness.

'That's not Ellen's knock, nor Jane's; she is not already back again. Besides, she also does not knock like that. Who is it?'

The knocking came again—slightly, more insistently than before.

'If it is some bothering visitors, they will have a short answer, I promise them. When I do not open, why do they not take a hint and go? I am not to be disturbed when I am making my arrangements to remain undisturbed for ever.'

The knocking was repeated for a third time.

'So, they persist! Well, I will show them. They shall see.'

Cramming her trio of treasures into the pocket of her dress, where one would have supposed them to be in uncomfortable, not to say dangerous, juxtaposition, she strode to the door, intent on scarifying the presumptuous caller. When, however, she perceived who stood without, surprise for the moment made her irresolute.

The visitor was Mr Horace Burton, at whom Miss Casata stared, as if he were the very last person she had expected to see—which, probably, as a matter of fact, he was. Mr Burton, on the other hand, bestowed on her his blandest smile. He sauntered past her as if he had not the slightest doubt in the world that he would be regarded as a welcome guest.

'Hollo, Lou! come to pay you a visit.'

His tone was light and airy, in striking contrast to her demeanour, which was about as tragic as it could be.

'Go! Do you hear me, go, before you are sorry, and I am sorry, too!'

Her manner seemed to leave him quite unmoved.

'Now, my dear girl, don't look at me like that; it isn't nice of you. I'm here as a friend—a friend, you understand—and something more than a friend.'

'You are no friend of mine; no, you never can be. I tell you again to go at once, or you will be sorry. I have warned you.'

'That's all right; you'll change your tone when you hear what I have to say. I've come here to bring sunshine into your life, to ask for your forgiveness, to undo the past. Be sensible; there's a good girl.'

'Sensible? Oh, yes, I will be sensible. There's someone else here.'

'Yes, that's Cox; he's a friend of mine. He's come here to see fair-play and witness my repentance. Come in, Cox.' Mr Thomas Cox entered, looking, if the thing were possible, less like a Thomas Cox than ever. 'Cox, let me present you to Miss Casata, the only woman I ever loved. There have been times when I have been forced to dissemble my love. Hang it, Cox! you know how I've been pressed. When a man's in such a hole as I've been in, he crushes down the love which he feels for a woman; he has to, if there's any manhood in him. He doesn't want to drag her down into the ditch in which he lies. But, Cox, you know how I have loved her all the time.'

Mr Burton turned away his head—whether to hide a tear or a smile was uncertain. He spoke with a degree of volubility which, under the circumstances, was remarkable. As Miss Casata appeared to think, her tone remained inflexible.

'There still is someone else.'

'Ah, that's the Flyman; he's nothing and nobody; he doesn't count. Let him have a chair, and he can wait in the hall, Lou, till you and I come to an understanding.'

Mr Burton's suggestion was carried out. A chair was taken into the little hall, on which the Flyman placed himself. How long he remained on it, when their backs were turned, was another matter. The outer door was closed, as also, Miss Casata having entered, was the door into the drawing-room. But that was of no consequence; the Flyman's ears were keen.

There was a curious glitter in the lady's eyes when she confronted her quondam lover. Now and then she touched her lips with the tip of her tongue, as if they were dry. Her hands continually opened and shut, apparently of their own volition. Occasionally one of them found its way into her pocket, feeling if her treasures still were there. She spoke as if her throat were sore.

'Well, what is it that you want? what new lie have you to tell?'

'I want to marry you; and, Lou, that's no lie.'

She was silent. One could see her bosom moving up and down. Then, becoming conscious of the two men's scrutiny, she drew herself up straighter, as if resolute to keep herself in hand.

'You insolent!'

'Insolent! Now, Lou, that's not nice of you. A man's not insolent who wants to marry the woman whom he loves, and who loves him.'

'I love you? I?' She tapped her chest with her forefinger. 'I love you so much that I would like to tear you to pieces! That is the sort of love I have for you. You—thing!'

'Lou, you're letting your temper get the better of you. I know I treated you badly.'

'Badly!'

She laughed—a mirthless little laugh.

'I know you've a right to feel annoyed with me—'

'Annoyed with you? Oh, no, not that!'

'But I was forced to do what I did; I couldn't help myself.'

'No doubt!'

'But now it's different altogether. I see things in a new light. I know what a mistake I've made. I've found out that I love you even more than I thought I did, and I've come to ask you to give me another chance—to forgive me. You're a woman, Lou, the best of women, and you've a forgiving heart; I know you have. Let me be your husband. I'll treat you better in the future; really, now!'

'What does all this mean?'

'It means what I say. Doesn't your own heart tell you so?'

'Oh, yes, it tells me. It tells me all sorts of things. It is a fool and a liar. It is of you I ask what does it all mean? It is you I want to tell me. Never mind what my heart says; we will leave my heart alone. I think we'd better.'

'Well, look here, I'll be candid. You're clear-sighted, whatever else you are, and level-headed; a cleverer woman I never met. I've told you so scores of times. With a woman of your type, candour's the best policy, as you say. So here's the matter in a nutshell. I'm in a hole; you're in a hole. You help me out of the hole I'm in; I'll help you out of the hole you're in. That's what I've come to say to you to-night. You appreciate frankness; there you have it.'

'What is the hole you are in?'

'My dear Lou, you know quite well. I've never kept it secret from you; I've always made you my confidant. What I want is my uncle's ruby. You tell me where it is, and help me to lay my hand upon it, and I'll marry you in the morning. And there's the proof that I mean what I say.'

He handed her an official-looking document, which purported to be an announcement of the fact that notice had been given to a certain registrar requiring him to perform the ceremony of marriage, by special licence, between Horace Burton and Louise Casata. The lady, however, scarcely glanced at it. She kept her eyes fixed on the gentleman.

'Your uncle's ruby!'

'That's it. As you know, if I can get it in my possession, it means fortune; if I can't, it may mean misfortune of a bad type. As I'm not taking any chances, if you'll help me to lay my hand on it, I'll marry you in the morning.'

'What a liar you are!'

'My dear Lou, all men are liars; somebody else said it before you. But where's the lie in this particular case? You've the proof in your hand that I mean business. Cox shall come with us and see it done. Won't you, Cox?'

Mr Thomas Cox bowed.

'Pleased to do anything to oblige a lady.'

'There you are! If you like, you needn't lose sight of me until we're married.'

'You say you want your uncle's ruby?'

'Of course, you know I do.'

'I know that you have it already.'

'I wish I knew as much. If I had it, I shouldn't be here to-night. There's another piece of candour.'

'I saw him take it.'

'Him? Who?'

'The man outside whom you call the Flyman. I saw him from a window take it last night from Mr Holland.'

Mr Burton turned to Mr Cox.

'There you are! There's one witness. How many more might there have been? The Flyman's a fool to transact a delicate piece of business of that description in a public thoroughfare!' He returned to Miss Casata. 'My dear Lou, you saw him try to take it, unfortunately without success.'

'He took everything Mr Holland had.'

'You appear to be well-informed upon the subject, though I don't know from what quarter your information comes. Still, what you say is pretty accurate. He did take all he could. He even took a ruby. Here it is for you to look at. Unluckily, it's not my uncle's. Hence these tears.'

He handed her the ruby signet ring which the Flyman, when he turned Mr Holland face downwards on the pavement, found that gentleman had been lying on.

CHAPTER XIV.
WHO KNOCKS?

Miss Casata examined the ring with every show of interest.

'This is the ruby he took from Mr Holland.'

'It is.'

'It is the only one which Mr Holland had.'

'So the Flyman said. He ought to know. I believe, on this occasion, he's no liar.'

'And it's not your uncle's?'

'It is not.'

'You are sure?'

'Dead.'

'Then, now I understand.'

'I wish I did share your understanding.'

'I understand why she laughed when he had gone, and why she said, "Poor Guy, how disappointed he will be!"'

'What is it you're talking about? Would you condescend to explain?'

'Yet—I do not understand. It was the box. Wait; in a second I will be back.'

She was back in less than a minute, bearing in her hand a small leather-covered box. On the lid was gummed a narrow strip of paper, on which was written, in delicate characters, 'The Burton Ruby.' Mr Burton received it with a cry of recognition.

'It's it; but the writing's strange.'

'It is her writing.'

'It's uncle's box—the one in which he always kept the blessed thing. There's his crest; there's where I dropped it in the ink.' He raised the lid. 'It's empty!'

'Last night Mr Holland took from it the ring which was inside. I always imagined that in it she kept your uncle's ruby, which was what I said to Mr Holland, as I told you I would do.'

'You're a nice girl, Lou!'

'And you're a nice man! Are you not a nice man?'

Mr Cox interposed.

'Now, don't let's have any quarrelling. Stick to business. Time's precious. Go on with your story.'

The lady turned and rent him.

'I will not go on with my story for you. What business of yours is my story, you dirty Jew?'

Mr Burton smiled benignly.

'Personalities! personalities! Don't call the man a Jew, my dear. Cox is no Jew; he's an anti-Semite. Continue your story for me, my love.'

Miss Casata complied with his request, although not in the most gracious manner.

'Do not call me your love, or you will be sorry. As Mr Holland was taking the ring out of the box, she came in—'

'And caught him at it? It must have been exciting. Wicked Guy!'

'He wished to give it to her back again, but she said, "Go, and take it with you." He took it, and went. Then, when he had gone, she began to laugh. She kept on laughing—it was true laughter, not false—as if it was the best joke in the world, and she said, "Poor Guy, how disappointed he will be!"'

'You notice things.'

'I am not a fool.'

'Is it possible that anyone ever mistook you for one?'

Mr Cox dug him with his elbow in the ribs, by way of a hint to him to hold his tongue. Miss Casata went contemptuously on,—

'I perceive now that she laughed because she knew that he had not taken with him what he supposed; but what I do not understand is, where, then, is the ring? I know she kept it in this box.'

She examined minutely the one she held. Mr Cox put a question to Mr Burton.

'For the last time, Burton, I suppose you're quite sure that it's not your uncle's ring? Nice we should look if it was afterwards discovered that you had made a mistake.'

'Don't be a silly ass! How many more times do you want to hear me swear? I say, Cox, have you two legs, or four, and which end of you are they? I might just as reasonably put such questions to you. I tell you, I know.'

Miss Casata was still continuing her scrutiny.

'It is not the ring; you are right. It is not the ring which she used to keep in the box. The stone in that, I think, was larger. It had a crest on it, I remember. And inside there was a name engraved, "George Burton." She showed it me one day, and she said, "I shall have to have this stone remounted. I cannot wear a man's name upon my finger, especially that man's name." I remember very well. Oh, no, this is not the ring at all.'

Mr Burton turned in triumph to Mr Cox. 'You hear? Now, who's right?'

'You have seen the ring which you describe?'

'It is certain; more than once. When was the last time? Not many days ago. It was in this box. She took it out of this box, she put it back into the box, and the box she put into the little bottom drawer. I remember it very well. When I heard of Mr Burton's will, I thought of it at once.'

'Then where is it now?'

'She must have taken it out of the box and put it somewhere else.'

'But where? Think!'

'How do I know? how can I think? She must have put it with some of her other jewels. They are everywhere—all over the place.'

Mr Cox and Mr Burton exchanged glances. The young gentleman took up the running.

'In that case, we'll look for it all over the place.'

'What do you mean?'

'My dear Lou, I'm going to have that ruby, and before I leave these premises. So, now, you've got it.'

'You will not touch her things?'

'I've no desire to do anything so indelicate. You tell us where it is, or give us a hint.'

'I have not the slightest notion.'

'Then we'll investigate for ourselves.'

'You shall not touch her things!'

'Lou, you gave Guy Holland the tip. You helped him to commit a burglary. Why should you be squeamish now?'

'That was different.'

'Of course it was. He's not attached to you like I am; he doesn't worship the ground you stand upon. It isn't as though you were smitten with Miss Bewicke, because you're not; you've told me so a hundred times. She's going to play some pretty trick on her own account; that's the meaning of her taking out the ruby, which she knew you knew was in that box. And it's a thousand to nothing that she means to play it at my expense. If I can help it, I don't mean to let her have the chance. Your fortune's bound with mine; we sink or swim together. If I don't get that ruby, and to-night, it'll probably mean that I go under, and, if I go, you'll go too. My dear girl, you know you will. Come, be sensible; be something like your dear own self. Do only half for me what you did for Guy. Let me just have a look round for that wretched ruby. By your own account, it must be somewhere close at hand. I'm sure to get it, and, when I do get it, I'll not forget the part you played. It'll not be my fault if I don't still make you the best husband a woman ever had.'

'I was not here when Mr Holland came. I did not see what he did. I knew nothing.'

'You need not see what we do. We have a little something somewhere which will make you as unconscious of anything that may take place as you can possibly desire. Then, if there is a bother, you will be able to assume, with perfect propriety, the *rôle* of injured victim. But I don't see that there need be trouble, if you keep still. I've as much right to that ruby as anybody else. I'm going to assert that right, that's all. Now, be a good, kind girl. Go into another room and have a nice little read. We're going to have a ruby hunt. Flyman!'

The Flyman appeared at the open door. At sight of him, Miss Casata broke into a storm of exclamations.

'Not him! He shall not come in here. He killed Mr Holland! I saw him! Mr Holland's blood is on his hands! I will not have that he come in here!'

'My dearest girl, but that's absurd. He's the only one of the three who understands locks. You don't want us to irretrievably ruin Miss Bewicke's property owing to our sheer want of skill? And for a nose for such a trifle as that ruby we are hunting for he has not his equal. Now, you go and have a nice little read.'

He moved forward with the possible intention of taking her by the arm and leading her from the room. If such was his design, it failed. As he advanced, she slipped past him. Rushing to the door which led into Miss Bewicke's bedroom, she placed herself in front of it. She took out one of the three treasures which were in her pocket—the revolver. Before the three men had even dreamed that she might be in possession of such a weapon, it was pointed at their heads. Her tone when she spoke was as significant as her attitude.

'If one of you tries to come through this door, I will shoot him dead. Do not think this revolver is not loaded. I will show you.'

She fired, the bullet penetrating the opposite wall. Mr Thomas Cox ducked as it passed. His companions instinctively shrank back. Her lips parted in a grim smile. Apparently this was her idea of humour.

'You see I am not so helpless as you perhaps supposed. I am not nervous, not at all. I am used to handle a revolver. I have won prizes for pistol shooting, oh, several times. There are five more barrels which are loaded. If I aim at you, I promise that I will not miss. You shall see.'

The bearing of the trio, in its way, was comical, they were evidently so completely taken by surprise. Mr Thomas Cox, in particular, looked as if this were an expedition in which, under the circumstances, he wished he had not taken part. He said as much.

'Look here, Burton, this is more than I bargained for. Before we came I told you that I was not going to be mixed up with anything equivocal. I have my character to consider. You said your lady friend would listen to reason; if your lady friend won't listen to reason, then I'm sorry, but I'm off.'

'Then you'll lose your money.'

'In that case you'll have to smart for it.'

'That won't give you your money. It's a nice little lot.'

'I know it's a nice little lot, and I can't afford to lose it; you know I can't afford to lose it. But there's something I can afford to lose still less, and that—that's my character.'

'Your character! Why, if you only could manage to get rid of your character—I don't believe you yourself realise what an awful one it is—it'd be the best stroke of business you've done for many a day, my dear Cox!'

Mr Burton advanced, as if to tap his friend, in an affable manner, on the shoulder. This brought him within a few feet of where Miss Casata was standing. Laying his left hand on Mr Cox's shoulder, with his right he snatched away that gentleman's walking-stick, swung round and struck Miss Casata's outstretched wrist with such violence that the revolver was driven from her grasp and sent flying across the room. She gave a cry of pain. Her arm fell limp at her side. The blow had been delivered with so much force that it was quite possible her wrist was broken.

'You devil!'

'You wild cat!' returned the gentleman. 'Now, Flyman, on to her!'

The Flyman obeyed. The two gentlemen attacked the lady. Although she fought gamely, especially considering her injured wrist, she was no match for the pair. They got her down upon the floor, still struggling for all that she was worth.

'Now, Flyman, where's that stuff of yours?'

'I'm getting it. She's a oner. She's bit me to the bone.'

With difficulty—he only had one hand disengaged— he evolved a tin canister from his jacket pocket.

'Bite her to the bone! Let her have the lot!'

From the canister the Flyman managed to take a cloth—a cloth which was soaked with some peculiar-smelling fluid. This he jammed against the lady's face, even cramming it between her lips. She writhed and twisted, then lay still.

As the Flyman got up, he examined the hand which she had marked with her teeth.

'She takes a bit of doing. I shouldn't like to have to tackle her single-handed.'

Mr Burton smiled. His clothes were a little rumpled. As he rose he arranged his tie.

'Nice wife she'd make! What do you think?'

Mr Cox had occupied his time in picking up the revolver of which the lady had been relieved. He seemed genuinely concerned.

'You know, Burton, I tell you again I didn't come here for this sort of thing. I wouldn't have had this happen not—not for a good deal. I shouldn't be surprised if we get into trouble for this.'

'My dear Cox, we should have got into trouble anyhow. We may as well be hung for a sheep as a lamb. I'm going for the gloves.'

'Hung! Don't talk about hanging. You make a cold shiver go down my back. You haven't—killed her?'

'Killed her? You innocent! She's the sort who take a deal of killing. My good chap, when she comes to, she'll curse a little and go on generally; but she'll forgive me in the end. I know her; she's a dear!'

While the three men stood looking down at the unconscious woman, there came a knocking at the outer door.

CHAPTER XV.
AN HONOURABLE RETREAT

It was not what they expected. Their faces showed it; they were so unmistakably startled. They looked at each other, then at the unconscious woman, then back again at one another. Mr Burton bit his lip.

'Who the deuce is that?'

'Servants, perhaps.'

'The suggestion was the Flyman's.'

'Then confound the servants! Why can't they take a little extra time to-night? They know their mistress is away.'

The knocking came again—a regular rat-tat-tat.

'That's no servants. They wouldn't make that row.'

'You can never tell. Nowadays they make what row they please; they fancy themselves. Brutes!'

'Visitors, perhaps.'

'Confound them, whoever it is!'

They spoke in whispers, an appreciable pause between each man's speaking, as if each in turn waited for something to happen. Mr Burton was outwardly the most self-possessed, being the kind of man who would probably smile as he mounted the gallows. The Flyman had his eyes nearly shut, his fists clenched, his shoulders a little hunched, as if gathering himself together to resist a coming attack. Mr

Thomas Cox was visibly tremulous; his great head twitched upon his shoulders; he was apparently in danger of physical collapse. It was curious to observe the contrasting attitudes of the three men as they stood about the recumbent woman.

The knocking was repeated, still more loudly, as if the knocker waxed impatient.

'We shall have to let 'em in. Anyhow, we shall have to see who's there. They'll knock the door down.'

This was the Flyman. Mr Cox suggested an alternative.

'Can't we—can't we get away? Isn't there another way out?'

Mr Burton enlightened him.

'My dear Cox, there's only one way into a flat, and there's only one way out, unless you try the window, which means a drop of perhaps a hundred feet. I'm not dropping. The Flyman's right; we shall have to see who's there. There needn't be trouble, unless you give yourself away. It depends who it is. I'll lay this dear little girl of mine upon her bed; she'll be more comfortable there, and not so conspicuous. I know which is her room. Then we'll see who's come to call on you.'

Displaying a degree of strength with which one would hardly have credited his slight figure, lifting Miss Casata off the floor, he bore her from the room. During his absence there came the knocking for the fourth time, this time furiously. When he returned, a marked change had taken place in his appearance. There were signs of strange disorder on his countenance, as if during his brief withdrawal he had been unstrung by some overwhelming shock. The Flyman at once observed his altered looks.

'What's happened? What's the matter?'

'Curse you, Flyman!'

'What have I done now?'

'I say, curse you!'

'Is she—dead?'

'No, she's not. I'm going to open the door. If it's the servants, I'll send them away, pretending to give them a message from her; if it's callers, I'll tell them a lie; if it's anybody who wants to make himself unpleasant, you two look out. I'm not going to be bluffed out of this before I've got that ruby.'

'Burton, be careful what you do, for all our sakes.'

This was Mr Cox. The retort was hardly courteous.

'You be hanged!'

Mr Burton reached the front door as the knocking was recommencing. From where they were they could not see what he did, but they could hear. They heard him open; a feminine voice inquire, in tones of indignation,—

'What's the meaning of this? Why am I kept waiting?'

Then the front door slammed, the drawing-room door was thrown violently open, and two young ladies came through it, one after the other, with such extremely indecorous rapidity as to suggest that they could scarcely be entirely responsible for their own proceedings, as, indeed, they were not. Mr Horace Burton had propelled them forward with his own right arm before they themselves had the least idea what was about to happen. And, following right upon their heels, he closed the drawing-room door, turned the key and stood with his back against it, surveying them with his habitual, benignant smile.

It was what they call upon the stage a tableau, The smiling gentleman, the two bewildered ladies, the two other almost equally bewildered men, for it was an open question which were the more surprised by the singularity of Mr Burton's behaviour—Miss Bewicke and Miss Broad or Mr Thomas Cox and the Flyman.

The peculiar nature of her reception seemed to have driven Miss Broad's wits completely from her. She gazed around like a woman startled out of sleep, who has no notion of what has roused her. Miss Bewicke had apparently retained some fragments of hers. She looked at Mr Burton, then at Mr Cox and the Flyman, then back at the gentleman who stood before the door. She eyed him up and down with a mixture, as it seemed, of amusement, anger and contempt. Could a voice have stung, hers would have stung him then. But this gentleman was pachydermatous.

'So it's you?'

'I guess it is.'

'How dare you come here?'

'That's the problem.'

'It's one which will soon be solved.'

She moved across the room. He checked her.

'It's no good your ringing the bell. There's no one to answer.'

As she turned to face him, Miss Broad spoke, with an apparent partial return to consciousness.

'Who is this person?'

'This person is Horace Burton, of whom you may have heard. I cannot tell you who the other persons are. They look as if they were friends of his.'

'So this is Horace Burton?'

Miss Broad regarded the gentleman in question as if he were some unclean thing, which, possibly, she considered him to be. He, on the other hand, continued genial as ever.

'And you're Miss Broad—Letty, I believe? I'm pleased to meet you, cousin that is to be.'

'Cousin—your cousin? I shall never be a cousin of yours.'

'No? That's hard on Guy. He's counting on the money.'

'You despicable creature!' She turned away, presenting him with a good view of her back, and put a question to Miss Bewicke. 'What is he doing here? Surely you don't allow him in your rooms?'

Mr Burton took upon himself to answer for the lady.

'I'll tell you what I'm doing here; she can't. I'm now for the first time going to tell her also. It'll be giving her a little piece of information which I know she'll value. Miss Bewicke, I've come here in search of a quarter of million of money.'

'Is that so? You really are too modest! It was surely scarcely worth your while to come for such a trifle! I need hardly say that you will find several little sums of that amount lying loose about the premises!'

'Indeed? Well, I want one; that's all.'

'Mr Burton, will you be so good as to leave my rooms?'

'I'll leave them on the wings of the wind, whatever that may be, when I have my uncle's ruby.'

'When you have what?'

'My uncle's ruby. My dear cousin Guy committed burglary here last night in quest of it, so I'm sure you won't mind my paying you a little call this evening as a sort of sequel.'

'I suppose Louise Casata told you about Mr Holland?'

'There's no charge for supposing.'

'Probably the same person also informed you that he went away with what he sought?'

'Did he, Miss Bewicke?'

'You had better refer to your informant.'

'I'm referring to you. I'm asking you if Guy Holland left these rooms last night in possession of my uncle's ruby?'

'Ask Miss Casata; ask your cousin even, but don't ask me.'

'I am asking you. You've been playing some confounded trick.'

'Mr Burton!'

'I don't wish to hurt your feelings, Miss Bewicke, so I'll say you've been amusing yourself with some dainty, delicate device, and I shouldn't be surprised to learn that you have that ruby on your person at this moment.'

Miss Bewicke, walking to the bell, pressed her finger against the button, so that it kept up a continuous ringing. Mr Burton watched her with a smile.

'You see, there's no one there. You might have taken my word.'

'Where is Miss Casata?'

'Where is she? That's the question. Where's everyone?'

'If I am unable to attract the attention of my own servants, thanks to you, my friends in the next flat will hear the unceasing tinkling of the bell, and guess that there is something wrong.'

'I should be sorry, Miss Bewicke, to have to seem rude to a lady—'

'On the contrary, I should imagine that few things would give you greater pleasure; you are that kind of person.'

'At the same time, I must request you to leave that bell alone.'

He went closer to her. His moving away from it left the door unguarded. Over her shoulder she shot a glance at Miss Broad. That young lady, catching it, perceived the little ruse she had been playing. Hurrying to the door, she began to turn the key, and had already unlocked it when Mr Burton came rushing back to the post which he had been beguiled into deserting.

'You darling!' he cried.

Seizing Miss Broad by the waist he dragged her from the door. As he whirled her round, she struck him with her clenched fist on his right ear, the blow being delivered with such good judgment, force and fortune that it carried the young gentleman clean off his feet and right over on to his back.

'Bravo!' exclaimed Miss Bewicke. 'Now, Letty, open the door!'

But Miss Bewicke was a little hasty in supposing that the road was free. As Mr Burton fell, he prevented Miss Broad from moving by clutching at her skirts. She struggled to release herself in vain; he gripped too tight. And the Flyman, hastening to occupy the fallen hero's place, confronted Miss Bewicke as she advanced.

'It's no good,' he observed. 'There's no road this way.'

She was not to be baffled without an effort.

'If you'll let me pass, I'll give you—'

'You won't give me anything, because you won't pass. Now, don't you be silly, or you'll be sorry. You won't bowl me over with a clip on the ear from your little fist.'

This was said because, encouraged, perhaps, by Miss Broad's success, Miss Bewicke showed signs of actual violence. The apparent recognition, however, of some peculiar quality on the face of the man in front of her caused her to relinquish her purpose, if it was ever formed. Instead, turning to Miss Broad, she took her by the hand.

'Come, quick!' she cried.

Mr Burton, reassured by the Flyman's arrival, loosed the lady's skirt as he ascended to his feet. The quick-witted proprietress of the rooms, taking instant advantage of Miss Broad's freedom, rushed her towards the door through which, not long since, he had carried Miss Casata. Divining their purpose, he tore after them as soon as he had regained his perpendicular.

'Stop them, you fools! Move yourself, Cox!'

But Mr Cox did not move himself. He remained motionless where he was standing, and Mr Burton, in spite of his impetuosity, was too late. They were not only through before he reached the door, but had banged it in his face, and turned the key on the other side. He shook the handle in vain.

'Open, you cats!'

They were not likely to comply with his civil invitation. He addressed himself to Mr Cox, on his face, all at once, a very peculiar look of pallor.

'I shouldn't be surprised if you swing for this.'

'Swing? For letting them through that door? Who do you think you're talking to?'

'I'm talking to you, my friend. What's the betting that your letting them through that door doesn't turn out a hanging matter for you? I'll take short odds.' He turned to the Flyman. 'Let me through there. There's another way into where they are; I'll see if I can get at them. You stay here, in case they try to double. Cox is no good. I'll be even with him for this.'

Mr Burton crossed to a door, which was on the other side of the little hall. Unlocked, it admitted him to the kitchen. From the kitchen he passed to another room, apparently where the servants slept. On the opposite side of this was still another door. He eyed it.

'If I remember rightly, that leads into her room.'

The door was locked; the key was in the lock upon the other side. He stooped to see; it was in a position which prevented anything being visible. He rattled the handle; rapped with his knuckles at the panel, without result. All was silent.

'It is her room. I wonder what they're up to? They're very still. They can't—'

He stopped, probably because the stillness of which he spoke was broken by a woman's cry—a mingling of surprise, anguish, fear. He retraced his steps towards the kitchen, whispering to himself two words,—

'They have!'

Taking the key from one side of the lock, replacing it in the other, he locked the door of the servants' room behind him. The key itself he pocketed.

'Except through the drawing-room, there's only this way out, so we've trapped you anyhow.'

As if to make assurance doubly sure, he locked the door of the kitchen also. Again he pocketed the key.

CHAPTER XVI.
THE FINDING OF THE RUBY AND THE LOCKING OF THE DOOR

When Mr Burton returned to the drawing-room, he found that Mr Thomas Cox had been having a few words with the Flyman. That worthy jerked his thumb in the other's direction.

'Wants to sling his hook. Says he's had about enough of it.'

'Oh, he has, has he? Now, Cox, listen to me. It's through you we're here—'

Interrupting, Mr Cox raised his hat and stick in a hasty disclaimer.

'Was there ever anything like that? It was your suggestion entirely. You said you could twist your lady friend round your finger—'

'Let's go a little further back, my Cox. You've told me—how many times?—that if I lose my uncle's money you'll send me to gaol. Not being anxious to go to gaol, I'm doing my best to get my uncle's money. So if it's not through you I'm here, I should like to know through whom it is.'

'That's different; you're entering on other matters altogether. You've committed—you know what you've committed; but it doesn't follow, because you've brought yourself within the reach of the criminal law, that I want to bring myself too.'

'You hand over those pieces of paper which you're always flicking in my face, and you're at liberty to go through that door, and down the stairs, and neither the Flyman nor I will ever breathe a word about your having been connected with the evening's entertainment.'

'Do you take me for a fool? You've robbed me on your own account already, and now you want to jockey me into robbing myself. Don't talk to me like that!'

'No, I won't talk to you like that; I'll talk to you like this. What there'll be to pay for this evening's proceedings I don't know; but you'll pay your share, whatever it is. This is a game of share and share alike, and of in for a penny in for a pound. The Flyman and I are going to see this through. I'm going to have the ruby before I leave, I tell you that; and you're going to be in with us right along.'

'Burton, you're a villain!'

'Cox, you're a scoundrel! Any use our saying pretty things to each other, you renegade Jew?'

Mr Cox was wiping his forehead with his pocket-handkerchief, as if he felt the heat.

'I will not be spoken to like that, as if I were—as if I were a man of your own type. Where—where have those women gone?'

'The room on the other side that door is the dining-room; beyond is Casata's room. That's where they've gone.'

'Then—then they've found her?'

'Oh, yes, they've found her; not a doubt of it. They've found a good many other things as well.'

His tone evidently struck Mr Cox as being disagreeably significant.

'For goodness' sake, Burton, let's go. You are so rash, don't let's make bad worse. Let's go while we have a chance, and before anything very serious has happened.'

'Something serious has happened.'

'What do you mean?'

'What I say.'

'You don't mean—'

'Oh, cut it! Flyman, Cox is too fond of cackle. We're losing valuable time, my child. You stay where you are, and keep an eye on things, while Cox and I find my uncle's ruby.'

The Flyman proposed an amendment.

'Excuse me, Mr Burton, but, if you don't mind, we'll have it the other way about. You stay here, and Mr Cox and I will find the ruby.'

Mr Burton laughed.

'Flyman, Doubt was your sire, out of Suspicion. Still think I want to do you?'

'Sure.' The Flyman drew his finger across his lips. 'Mr Burton, you're cleverer than most, and a lot cleverer than me. If you once got that there stone between your fingers, I might whistle for my thousand, and keep on whistling. Besides, I am handier than you at looking for a thing like that.'

'Then show your handiness; only look alive about it. We can't expect to continue in the enjoyment of these charming rooms for ever.'

'Where shall I start looking?'

'There you are, displaying your handiness from the very beginning. How am I to know? I'm not informed as to where she keeps her gewgaws. I believe that the pretty lady's sleeping-chamber is on the other side of that door; look, there.' The Flyman looked in the direction referred to. 'Hold hard; take Cox with you.'

The Flyman gripped Mr Thomas Cox by the arm.

'You come with me.'

Mr Cox objected.

'None of your handling.'

'Who wants to handle you? You come with me, that's all.'

'Yes, Cox, that's all. You go and assist our friend in prising open the pretty lady's jewel-boxes and dressing-cases, and so on. You know quite well that it isn't the first time you've been at the game, dear boy.'

'I'll have no finger in anything of the kind; and as for your imputations, I'll make you regret them, Mr Burton.'

'You will, will you? Take care, Cox; I'm in a nasty mood. If you won't take a hand in this game, we'll play it in spite of you. We'll count you out. Not a farthing shall you have of my money, and I defy you to put the law into execution against me. You know you daren't—now. The moment you move, I'll give the police the office to keep an eye on Thomas Cox. You've more to lose than we have.'

'You—you brutes! Don't try to bully me.'

'Bully? I don't bully, Cox. Here, I'll open that door, and you shall go through it at once, if you please. Only I'll go with you, and at the foot of the stairs I'll denounce you for murder. If the game is lost, as it will be if you won't play it out, I don't care if I do hang, so long as you hang with me.'

'What—what the devil do you mean by keeping on dropping hints about—about murder?'

'You shall know, if you like, when you reach the foot of the stairs. Take my earnest and well-meant advice, keep in with us, and take my word for it that each moment you waste brings the shadow of the gallows just a little nearer. I'll give you all the explanations you want afterwards, if there ever is an afterwards.'

Mr Cox hesitated. He glanced from one of his companions to the other. What he saw on their faces seemed to have on him an odd effect. He went with the Flyman into

Miss Bewicke's bedroom, looking as if he had all at once grown older. Mr Burton followed them with his eyes, the peculiar expression of his countenance seeming to endow his stereotyped smile with an unusual prominence. He looked, as he had said of himself, in a nasty mood.

'Leave the door open, Flyman. I also am interested in the proceedings, and should like to be instantly informed when you do light upon my uncle's precious jewel.'

He watched for a moment or two the Flyman pulling open such drawers as were unlocked and turning over their contents.

'Don't trouble yourself to look at the frills and laces. Women don't keep jewels among their underwear. Turn your attention to the dressing-table, man.'

The Flyman resented the comment on his mode of procedure.

'You never know where a woman does keep her things, especially the thing you're after, as you'd know if you'd as much experience as I have.'

Mr Burton, laughing, lit a cigarette.

'All right, man of many felonies. You're quite justified in resenting the criticism of the amateur. I was only telling you what was my own idea. Only do be quick and illustrate the handiness of which you bragged.'

He strolled towards the door which was on the opposite side of the room, the one through which the ladies had vanished. He softly tried the handle; it still was locked. Taking the cigarette from between his lips, he inclined his ear towards the panel and listened.

'They're quiet. I suppose they're in her room. I wonder what they're doing? Problem for the papers which give prizes for puzzles. Under the circumstances, what might they be expected to be doing? Odds on that they're doing something else. One might easily see. It wouldn't take long to cut a piece out of this panel, or, for the matter of that, to take the lock itself clean off. But would it be worth one's while? They've seen enough. Ye whales and little fishes, they've seen too much! Better carry the thing to a conclusion without unnecessary witnesses. If they're content, we are. What's up now?'

The question was prompted by an exclamation which came from Miss Bewicke's bedroom. Mr Cox appeared at the entrance.

'Burton, you said that all we wanted was the ruby; that the rest of her things should go untouched.'

'Well?'

'The Flyman's pocketing her jewels.'

Mr Burton crossed the floor.

'That won't do, Flyman. We're here on an expedition of right. We're not thieves.'

'You said yourself we might as well be hung for a sheep as a lamb.'

'I did; and you are aware that that is not the kind of sheep I meant. On this occasion I really must ask you to be honest.'

'But I never saw such shiners. Who could resist them, guv'nor? She's got enough to stock a shop. Why, if we take 'em away with us, we sha'n't be far out, even if we don't get that blessed ruby.'

'It's the ruby or nothing; also, and nothing. Put those things back.'

'I've only nobbled one or two. I've got to look after myself.'

'I, too, have to look after you. You know what was agreed; keep to the terms of the agreement, or, though you "nobble" every "shiner" the lady owns, you'll be a loser. Put those things back.'

There was something about Mr Burton just then which compelled respect, of a kind, which fact the Flyman recognised. His face darkened and, in audible tones, he grumbled. But he produced the trinkets, as requested, and replaced them, one by one, on their velvet beds.

'Is that all?'

'Every blooming one.'

'Cox, is that all?'

'Yes, I believe it is.' He glanced at the open jewel-case. 'No, there's a ring still missing.'

The Flyman cursed.

'Can't a bloke have one?'

'Not unless he wishes to pay for it more than it's worth. Come, man, look pleasant.'

The Flyman did not 'look pleasant;' but he restored the ring. Mr Burton expressed approval.

'That's better. Now, show yourself as keen in the right direction. Give us a proof of the "handiness" you talked about, and find that ruby. It'll be worth to you more than all those other things.'

On this point the Flyman, from his manner, seemed to have his doubts; but he continued his researches. Mr Cox observed that they were strictly confined to what Mr Burton had called the 'right direction.' Mr Burton, returning to the locked door, pursued his meditations as he listened at the panel.

'It's odd that they're so quiet, and suggests mischief. In such a case, surely women are not quiet. Unless—unless what? That's what I should like to know.'

'Burton, is this the ruby?'

The words came sharply from Mr Cox, with a sudden interposition from the Flyman.

'You give me that! Don't you lay your fingers on the thing!'

'I'm only looking at it.'

'You give it me, I say.'

'Burton!'

The cry was almost an appeal for help. Mr Burton arrived to find something very like a tussle taking place. The Flyman was endeavouring to obtain possession of something which Mr Cox was holding, and which that gentleman was doing his best to keep.

'I found it!' he cried. 'Hand it over!'

'Burton! Quick! Catch!'

Mr Cox tossed something through the air which Mr Burton caught. He had just time to see that it was a ring, set with a gleaming red stone, when the Flyman was upon him with an emphatic repetition of the demand he had made on Mr Cox.

'You hand it over before I down you.'

Mr Cox explained.

'I found it; he didn't. I opened the box, and it was the first thing I saw. It had nothing to do with him.'

The Flyman paid no attention to the statement. He merely reiterated his request.

'Now, Mr Burton, I don't want no patter. You fork up before there's trouble.'

The young gentleman, holding his hand behind his back, was smiling in the other's face.

'Gently, Flyman. Let's know exactly where we are before we come to business.' The Flyman flung himself upon him without another word. Mr Burton never for a moment seemed to lose his self-possession. 'You ass! what do you suppose you're going to gain by this?'

While they struggled, the bedroom door was suddenly slammed to. There was a clicking sound. The continuation of the argument was instantly deferred. Mr Burton hurried to the door.

'They've caught us napping; it's locked. Well, Flyman, I hope you're satisfied. Owing to your "handiness," of which we have heard so much, in our turn we are trapped.'

CHAPTER XVII.
THE FIGURES ON THE BED

'At anyrate,' remarked Miss Bewicke, as, turning the key in the lock, she shut herself and Miss Broad inside the dining-room, 'you can't get at us for a time.'

The two girls stood and listened. They heard the handle tried; the rapping at the panel.

'You may knock, and knock, but it won't be opened. He's gone. That was Horace, dear. How beautifully you knocked him down!'

'What does he want?'

'It's pretty plain. Uncle George's ruby has the attractiveness of the Holy Grail. This is another quest for it.'

'But they'll find it if we stop here.'

'And if we don't stop here, what do you propose to do? Fight them to the death? Nothing else will be efficacious. They're not the persons, and they're not in the mood, to stick at trifles.'

'What a wretch he is! I've heard Guy speak of him, but I'd no idea he was as bad as this.'

'My dear Letty, when a bad man is in a bad hole, you've no notion how bad that man can be. The question now is,

163

Can we get out through the kitchen door, or can they get through the kitchen door to us?'

'Where does that door lead to?'

'Into Louise Casata's bedroom. The beauty of the average flat is that you can always pass from any one room into any other, which, sometimes, is convenient and sometimes isn't. I'm wondering whether Louise is responsible for Horace Burton's presence here, and also where she is. I've reasons for believing that it was not her intention to go out to-night.'

'I shouldn't keep such a woman about my place, if I were you.'

'I don't intend to any longer. All the same, you've no idea how useful she has been. There have been times when I don't know what I should have done without her. Still, I fancy that henceforth she and I part company.' She opened the door which led into Miss Casata's room, then gave utterance to a startled exclamation. 'Why! what is the matter? Letty, keep back!'

Returning to the dining-room, she leaned against the door, which she had pulled to after her, as if she needed its support. For one who was, as a rule, so completely mistress of herself, she showed strange emotion. Miss Broad stared at her askance.

'What has happened now? What's in there?'

'I don't know. Don't ask me. Let me get my breath and think, and I'll tell you all about it.'

She pressed her hand against her side, as if to still the beating of her heart. She seemed unhinged, thrown, in a second, completely off her balance. Her agitation was infectious. Probably, without her knowing it, Miss Broad's voice trembled and sank.

'Tell me—what it is.'

'Wait a minute, and I'll tell you—all.'

She made an evident effort to get the better of her infirmity. Bracing herself up against the door, the little woman looked Miss Broad straight in the face.

'Letty, something horrible has happened.'

'What is it?'

'I don't quite know myself; I didn't stop to look.'

'Let me go and see.'

'It's Miss Casata and—a man.'

'A man? What man?'

'I can't say; I only saw it was a man. They're lying on the bed—so still. Oh, Letty!'

'May!'

Miss Broad was probably wholly unaware that she had called her companion by her Christian name. The unknown horror in the other room had laid its grip on her. She was overcome by frightful imaginings, not knowing why. She gasped out an unfinished question.

'You don't mean—'

'I don't know what I mean. I only know that there's something there.'

The two girls had been speaking in whispers, as if they stood in a presence which compelled hushed voices. Now, suddenly, Miss Bewicke raised her tones, extending her small palm towards the door through which they had entered.

'Oh! you wretches! wretches!'

She broke into a passion of tears.

'May, for goodness' sake, don't cry!'

'I'm not going to. I don't know why I am so silly, but, for the moment, I couldn't help it.' Her sobs ceased almost as rapidly as they came. She dried her eyes. 'Letty, let's go and see what's happened. I'm afraid Miss Casata's—dead.'

'Dead?'

'Yes; and—the man.'

'The man?'

'They're so still. Let's go and see. Give me your hand.'

Miss Broad yielded her hand. Miss Bewicke opened the door. The two peeped through.

The room was not a large one. On one side was an ordinary French bedstead. A brass railing was on the head and foot. On this railing were hung feminine odds and ends. These made it difficult for anyone standing at the door to see clearly what was on the bed. Miss Broad perceived that on the outer edge there lay a woman.

'Who's that?'

'That's Louise Casata.'

'Perhaps she's sleeping.'

'She wouldn't sleep through all the noise.'

'She may be ill; I'll go and look at her.'

'Don't you see—that there's a man?'

Miss Broad moved further into the room. She saw what the other alluded to. As she did so, she gave utterance to that cry which Mr Horace Burton heard, listening in the servants' room beyond—the cry in which there was such a mingling of emotions as they welled up to the lips from the woman's heart.

Miss Casata lay almost on the extreme edge of the bed fully clothed. She was on her back. One arm dangled over the side; her head was a little aslant upon the pillow, so that from a little distance it looked as if her neck was broken. The whole pose was almost as uncomfortable a one as a human being could choose; indeed, the conviction was irresistibly borne in on the beholders that it was not self-chosen, unless she had sunk on to the bed in a drunken stupor; but Miss Bewicke knew that she was no drinker.

However, it was not Miss Casata's plight which had drawn from Miss Broad that involuntary cry. Beside her, outlined beneath the bedclothes, was a figure, stiff and rigid. With the exception of one place, it was completely covered. Some one, curious, perhaps, to learn what the thing might mean, had drawn aside sufficient of the bedclothes to disclose a portion of the head and face. As a matter of fact, the curious person was Mr Horace Burton. When relieving himself of the burden of the lady who was once the object of his heart's affection, he had been struck by the outlined form which lay so curiously still, and had wondered what it was, and had seen; and because of what he had seen, had gone back to his companions with the fashion of his countenance so changed.

Now Miss Broad saw. The man beside Miss Casata on the bed was Mr Holland—Guy Holland—her Guy. It was when she perceived that it was he that her heart cried out. Miss Bewicke, who had only realised that it was a man, without recognising what man it was, came to her side trembling, wondering. When she also knew, she also cried aloud; but there was a material difference between the quality of her exclamation and Miss Broad's. Hers signified horror and amazement—perhaps something of concern; Miss Broad's betokened so many other things besides.

The two women went running to the bed; but when Miss Broad showed an inclination to lean over and to touch the silent man, the other, as if fearful of what actual contact might involve, caught her by the dress.

'No, no; take care!'

Even Miss Broad shrank a little back; for Miss Casata lay between.

'Move the bed!'

The suggestion was Miss Bewicke's. In a moment it had been put into force. The bed was wheeled more into the centre of the room, so as to permit of passage between it and the wall, and presently the girl was at her lover's side. She knelt and looked, but still she did not touch him. No tears were in her eyes; she seemed very calm; but her face was white, and she was speechless. On her face there was a look which was past wonder, past pain, past fear, as if she did not understand what it was which was in front of her. Miss Bewicke stood at her side, also looking; her dominant expression seemed sheer bewilderment.

He also lay on his back. The bedclothes were withdrawn, so that his face was seen down to the chin. No marks of violence were visible. His expression was one of complete quiescence. His eyes were closed, as if he slept; but if he did, it was very soundly, for there was nothing to show that he breathed.

Suddenly Miss Broad found her voice, or the ghost of it. Her lips did not move, and the words came thinly from her throat.

'Is he dead?'

The other did not answer; but, leaning over, she drew the bedclothes more from off him, and she whispered,—

'Guy!' They waited, but he did not answer. She called again, 'Guy!'

Yet no response. In that land of sleep in which he was, it was plain that he heard no voices.

The further withdrawal of the bedclothes had revealed the fact that he was fully dressed for dinner, as he was when Miss Bewicke had seen him last, the night before. His black bow had come untied; the ends strayed over his shirtfront, which was soiled and crumpled. His whole attire was in disarray. There were stains of dirt upon his coat. Now that they were so close, they perceived that traces of dry mud were on his face, as if it had been in close contact with the ground. About his whole appearance there was much which was ominous.

The fact that this was so seemed to make a fresh appeal to Miss Broad's understanding; probably to something else in her as well.

'Guy!' she cried.

Her tone was penetrating, poignant. If it did not reach the consciousness of him to whom she called, in another direction it had a curious and unlooked-for effect. As if in response to an appeal which had been made directly to herself, Miss Casata, on the opposite side of the bed, sat up. The girls clung to each other in startled terror. To them, for the moment, it was as if she had risen from the dead.

Although she had sat up, Miss Casata herself did not seem to know exactly why. She seemed not only stupid, but a little stupefied, and gasped for breath, her respirations resembling convulsions as she struggled with the after-effects of the narcotic. The two girls observed her with amazement, she, on her part, evidently not realising their presence in the least.

It was Miss Bewicke who first attained to some dim comprehension of the meaning of the lady's antics.

'She's been drugged; that's what it is. Louise!'

Miss Casata heard, although she did not turn her head, but continued to open and shut her mouth in very ugly fashion as she fought for breath.

'Yes; I'm coming. Who's calling?'

'I! Look at me! Do you hear? Louise!'

This time, if she heard, Miss Casata gave no sign, but, sinking back on the bed, clutched at the counterpane, making a noise, as she gasped for breath, as if the walls of her chest would burst.

'Letty, let me go! I must do something. She'll relapse, or worse, if we don't take care.'

Miss Bewicke hastened to the wash-handstand. Emptying a jug of water into a basin, she took the basin in her hands and dashed the contents, with what force she could, into the lady's face.

The salutation was effectual. Miss Casata floundered, spluttering, on to the floor, more like herself.

Miss Bewicke confronted her, the basin still in her hands.

'Who did that?'

'I did. Louise, wake up!'

Miss Casata seemed to be endeavouring her utmost to obey the other's command.

'What's the matter?'

'That's what I want to know. In particular, I want to know what is the meaning of Mr Guy Holland's presence in your room?'

'Holland?' She put her hand up to her head in an effort to collect her thoughts. She spoke as if with an imperfect apprehension of what it was she was saying. 'He was in the street—lying—on his face—so I brought him here—before the policeman came.'

'Before the policeman came? What do you mean? How did you know that he was lying in the street?'

'I saw—the Flyman—from the window—knock him down—he took the ruby.'

'The Flyman? Who is he?'

'A man—Horace knows—I knew—Horace had set him on. I didn't want him to get into trouble, so I brought him here. It was all I could do to carry him up the stairs—he was so heavy.'

'And do you mean to say you've had Mr Holland hidden in your room all day and night?'

'All day—and night. He's dead. The Flyman killed him. Horace will get into trouble—when it's known.'

Miss Casata, in her condition of semi-consciousness, said more than she had warrant for. Mr Holland was not dead. Even as she asserted that he was, he showed that her assertion was an error. While the still partly-stupefied woman struggled to get out of the darkness into the light, there came a cry from the white-faced girl on the other side of the bed.

'May, he moves!'

Startled into forgetfulness of what it was she held, Miss Bewicke dropped the slippery basin from her hands. It broke into fragments with a clatter. The noise of the shattered ware seemed actually to penetrate to Mr Holland's consciousness. Miss Bewicke would always have it that it was her breaking the basin which really brought him back to life. In an instant Miss Broad was half beside herself in a frenzy of excitement.

'May! May! he lives! Guy! Guy!'

Miss Bewicke, turning, saw that he was alive, but that, apparently, when that was said, one had said all.

CHAPTER XVIII.
REINFORCED

Mr Holland had opened his eyes; he had done nothing more. The movement might have been owing to an involuntary contraction of the muscles, so rigid did his attitude continue to be, so apparently unseeing were the staring pupils. But, for the instant, it was sufficient for Miss Broad that he had shown signs of volition even to so small an extent. She bent over the bed, addressing him by a dozen endearing epithets.

'Guy! My darling! my love! my dear! Don't you know me? It's Letty—your own Letty! Speak to me! Guy! Guy!'

But he did not speak. Nor was it possible, to judge from any responsive action on his part that he even heard. His continual unnatural rigidity cooled the first ardour of the lady's joy. She addressed Miss Bewicke. And now the tears were streaming down her cheeks.

'May, come here! Look at Guy! Get him to speak to me!'

To enforce compliance with her wish was not so easy, as Miss Bewicke saw, if the other did not. There was an uncanny look about Mr Holland's whole appearance which was not reassuring. He looked far indeed from the capacity for reasonable speech.

'He wants help. We ought to have a doctor at once.'

'Then fetch one—fetch one!'

That there was anything about the request which was at all unreasonable, seemingly Miss Broad did not pause to consider; she was too preoccupied with her own troubles and his. But to Miss Bewicke the difficulty of the errand forcibly occurred.

'You forget—' she began. Then stopped, for she remembered how easy it was, in the other's situation, to forget all things save one. She knit her brows and thought, the result of her cogitations being a series of disjointed sentences.

'They can hardly be such brutes, when they know. And yet it was they who put him there. I wonder! Do I dare?'

It seemed that she essayed her courage. She went to the door, and, for a moment, listened. Then turned the key, opened it an inch or two. What she saw and heard increased her valour, especially what she heard. The drawing-room was empty. Loud voices came through the open door of the bedroom—her own bedroom on the opposite side—sounds which did not speak of peace.

'I do believe they're fighting.'

She stole on tiptoe a foot or two into the empty room, then stopped in a flutter as of doubt—what might not happen if they caught her?—then tiptoed further, till she had reached the centre of the room. Again she paused. If she was seen, it was a long way back to the haven of comparative safety she had quitted. But the noise, if anything, grew louder. From some of the words which reached her, she judged it possible that they were too much occupied with their own proceedings to pay heed to anything else. She perceived that, by some stroke of good fortune, the key was outside the door. She screwed her courage to the sticking-point, forming a sudden resolution. Darting forward, thrusting the door to quickly, she turned the key, then, when the key was turned, the deed done, the three gentlemen trapped, she leaned against the wall, went white, seemed on the verge of fainting.

She went still whiter when the handle was turned within, and Mr Horace Burton's voice was heard demanding that the door be undone.

'If they should get out!'

The possibility of the thing, and the fear thereof, acted on her as a spur. She tore to the door which led out of the flat, and, throwing it open, almost fell into the arms of the cook and housemaid who were returning from their Sunday evening out. Seldom have domestic servants been more heartily welcomed. She addressed them by their names.

'Wilson! Stevens! go at once for the police!'

Instead of promptly obeying, they stared at her in astonishment. Her hat, which she had not removed during the lively incidents which had marked the passage of the time since her arrival home, was on one side, at that unbecoming angle which is a woman's nightmare; and there were other traces of disarray which were not in keeping with her best-known characteristics, for, with her, a pin misplaced was the thing unspeakable. While the cook and housemaid stared, hesitating to start, as they were bidden, in search of the representatives of law and order, the lift stopped at the landing, and from it, of all persons in the world, Mr Bryan Dumville emerged.

She flew into his arms, as, it may be safely said, she had never flown before.

'Oh, Bryan! Bryan! I'm so glad you've come!'

As the flattered gentleman was, no doubt, about to express his appreciation of the warmth of his reception, the lift commenced to descend. Something else occurred to her.

'Stop! stop!' she cried. The lift returned. The porter looked out inquiringly. 'Peters, there are thieves in my rooms! You had better come with us at once.'

'Thieves, miss? Hadn't I better—'

She cut the porter's sentence short, relentlessly.

'No, you hadn't. You must come with us at once. Don't you hear me say so?'

He went. They all went—the cook and the housemaid, the porter, Mr Bryan Dumville, and Miss May Bewicke. She went last. As she went, she shut the front and drawing-room doors behind her. She pointed towards her bedroom.

'They're in there at this moment—three of them.'

The porter seemed to have his doubts.

'Three of them? You're sure they are thieves, miss?'

'Am I sure? Why do you ask me such a question? Do you think I'm likely to make a mistake In a matter like that? Pray, don't be absurd.'

'In that case, if they are thieves, don't you think I'd better fetch the police?'

Miss Bewicke's wits worked quickly. Even when circumstances seemed against their working at all—since instructing the cook and housemaid to do as the porter was now suggesting that he should do—she had already been turning things over in her mind, with the result that she was not sure that she desired official assistance after all. If the police came, arrests would be made; she would have to see the thing through to the bitter end. In view of such a possible consummation, there were many points to be considered. Had she been an actress, with a keen eye for an advertisement—a type which, it is understood, does exist— the idea of figuring as the heroine of what the slang of the hour calls a 'cause célèbre' might have commended itself to her intelligence; but, as it happened, she was not that kind. If these gentlemen did come into the hands of the police— at anyrate, on this particular charge—it was possible that things might transpire which she, and possibly others, would not wish to have mentioned in court and in the papers. That the miscreants deserved all the punishment which the law might award them, she had no doubt whatever. At the same time, she was equally clear that they would duly, and shortly, receive their reward, if not at her instance, then at that of others. So, on the whole, she decided, in a twinkling, that she would take no final step till she saw which way the cat might jump.

'When I want you to fetch the police, I will tell you.' She turned to the housemaid. 'But there's one thing, Stevens, you might fetch, and must, and that's a doctor. Go to the nearest, and bring him at once.'

Even as she spoke, through the dining-room door there came three persons—Miss Broad, with Mr Guy Holland on her arm, looking the most woe-begone figure imaginable, but still alive, and plainly walking; behind them Miss Casata. For the second time Miss Bewicke countermanded her instructions.

'Stay, Stevens! Perhaps the doctor won't be wanted.'

CHAPTER XIX.
STILL WITH A SMILE

The five stared at the three, then, after momentary inspection, as if for the purpose of satisfying herself on certain points by visual inspection, Miss Bewicke moved towards Mr Holland.

'Oh, Guy, I am so glad to see you better! I do hope that you're all right.'

The words were, perhaps, a trifle banal, possibly because, for once, the nimble-witted lady was doubtful as to what was exactly the proper thing to say. Apparently, however, it was of little consequence what she said. The gentleman was still incapable of appreciating at their just value either words or phrases. That he knew she spoke to him was probable, for he turned and regarded her with vacant looks and glassy eyes; but that he realised who she was, or what she meant, was more than doubtful. Mumbled words proceeded from his stammering lips.

'All right—yes—quite all right—nothing wrong.'

Miss Broad looked at Miss Bewicke with eyes in which the tears still trembled. She appealed to her in a whisper, in tones which quivered.

'Won't you let them fetch a doctor?'

'Let them! Stevens, fetch the man at once.'

This time Stevens went in search of medical aid.

Mr Dumville had been observing Mr Holland with undisguised amazement. Now he clothed his thoughts with speech.

'Holland, what on earth's the matter with you? May, what does all this mean?'

Miss Bewicke explained; that is, she told as much as she thought it necessary and advisable that Mr Dumville should know in the fewest words at her command. Mr Dumville professed himself to be, what he plainly was, amazed. The tale was very far from being complete in all its details, or he would probably have been yet more surprised, in a direction, as things were, which he little suspected.

'And do you mean that that man Burton is still upon these premises?'

'He was in my bedroom, when I turned the key, with his two friends.' Mr Dumville strode forward. She caught him by the arm. 'What are you going to do?'

'Slaughter him!'

'I would rather you did not do that. It would make such a mess upon the floor.'

'Do you think that scoundrel's behaviour is a thing to laugh at? I'll show you and him, too, where the laughter comes in.'

'My dear Bryan, I know very well that there's nothing laughable about Mr Horace Burton or his proceedings. He is—oh, he's all sorts of things. I'd rather not tell you all the things I think he is.'

'I know.'

'Of course, you know. But, at the same time, when you have made sure that neither he nor either of his friends is taking away any of my property upon his person, I should be obliged if you would let them go.'

'Let them go! May, you're mad!'

'Believe me, Bryan, I am comparatively sane. I will tell you all my reasons later on. At present the thing is to get them gone. You may take my word for it that for Mr Horace Burton the day of reckoning is close at hand, and that it will be as terrible an one as even you can desire.'

'That won't be the same as if I'd killed him.'

'No, it won't be the same; it will be better. Could I creep between your arms if I knew that your hands were red with that man's blood? If you don't mind, as I locked the door, I'll open it. Please keep your hands off him as he comes out—for my sake, dear.'

She gave him a glance which possibly constrained him to obedience. She was famous in the theatre for the skill with which she used her eyes. Turning the key, throwing the bedroom door wide open, she stood before it with a little gesture of invitation.

'Pray, gentlemen, come out.'

And they came out, the hang-dog three, for, though each endeavoured to bear himself with an air of unconcern, in no case did the endeavour quite succeed. As regards Mr Thomas Cox, the failure was complete. He looked like nothing so much as the well-whipped cur which only asks to be allowed to take itself away with its tail between its legs. The Flyman, who was probably more habituated to positions of the kind, succeeded a trifle better. He looked defiance, as if he were prepared to match himself, at less than a moment's notice, against whoever came. Mr Horace Burton it was, however, who might claim to face the situation with the most imperturbable front. He looked about him, not jauntily so much as calmly, with his unceasing smile.

'More visitors, Miss Bewicke, I perceive. Ah! Guy, how are you? You're looking dicky. Louise, my dearest girl!'

Of its kind, his impudence was glorious. Mr Dumville strode up to him, as if forgetful of the lady's prohibition.

'By gad! I'd like to kill you!'

Mr Burton, glancing up at the speaker, did not turn a hair.

'I'm afraid I haven't the honour. Miss Bewicke, may I ask you to introduce me to the gentleman?'

'With pleasure. Mr Horace Burton, this is Mr Dumville. It is only at my urgent request that he refrains from breaking every bone in your body, as he easily could. But you know, and I know, that for you there's such a very bad time coming that I feel it's quite safe to leave you to the tender mercies of those to whom mercy is unknown. Turn out your pockets!'

'Charmed! I quite appreciate the motive which actuates your request, Miss Bewicke. Nothing could be more natural. But I give you my word of honour that neither of us has anything which belongs to you.'

Notwithstanding, Mr Burton turned his pockets inside out, smiling all the time. His companions followed suit, though scarcely with so much grace. So far as could be seen, neither of them was in possession of anything to which Miss Bewicke could lay claim, as she herself admitted.

'I really do believe you, Mr Burton, when you say that you—none of you—have property of mine. It sounds odd, and you may wonder why, but I do. Good-night.'

'Good-night I am indebted to you, Miss Bewicke, for a pleasant evening's entertainment.'

'Don't mention it. When the time comes to balance your accounts, you'll find the sum-total of your indebtedness altogether beyond your capacity to meet. Go.'

And they went. At least Mr Thomas Cox and the Flyman went—the first-named gentleman with an undignified rush, the second not very far from his heels; but Mr Burton lingered on the threshold to waft a kiss on his finger-tips to Miss Casata.

'Best love, Louise.'

The lady made a dash at him, inarticulate with rage.

'You—you!'

Miss Bewicke stayed her progress.

'Louise!'

Mr Burton laughed.

'My dearest girl, you can't expect to embrace me before all these people! Propriety forbids.'

When he had disappeared, Mr Dumville gave voice to his sentiments.

'I wish you'd let me kill him!'

Miss Bewicke nodded her head, with an air of the profoundest wisdom, as she laid her little hands on his two arms.

'My dear Bryan, before very long he'll be wanting to kill himself; that'll be so much nicer for us and so much worse for him.'

CHAPTER XX.
HOW THE CHASE WAS ENDED

Mr Samuel Collyer was seated in his office. Spread open on the table in front of him was Mr George Burton's will, which apparently he had just been studying. The study seemed to have afforded him amusement. Leaning back in his chair, he smiled. He referred to his watch.

'Twenty minutes past; they will soon be here. On these occasions, punctuality ought to be the rule, and generally is. George Burton was a curious man, and left a curious will. And yet I don't know. Why should I, or anyone, call it curious? By what right? When a man has neither wife nor children, and his only kindred are a couple of nephews to whom he is not particularly attached, surely he has a right to do as he likes with his own. It is his own—as yet. And if he chooses to attach to the succession certain conditions which appeal, we'll say, to his sense of humour, what title has anyone, lawyer or layman, to comment adversely on the expression of his wishes? So long as they are not in opposition to the general welfare of the body politic, it seems to me none. In a sense, most wills are curious, when you get right into them and understand their ins and outs. I daresay mine will be. I'm a bachelor. Upon my word, I don't know who has the best claim to the few pence I shall leave. Why shouldn't I ornament my testamentary dispositions with a few characteristic touches? Why not?'

While the lawyer propounded to himself this knotty problem, two visitors were shown in—Mr Holland, again upon Miss Broad's arm. He still was not himself. The effects of the sand-bag, which the Flyman had used with more enthusiasm than he had perhaps intended, had not yet all vanished. He seemed uncertain about his capacity to steer himself. He did not carry himself so upright as was his wont. There was a look upon his face which it had not previously worn—of indecision, irresolution, as if he was not quite master of his mental faculties. That sandbag had landed on the brain. Miss Broad seemed to regard him as if he were a child; she watched over him as if he were one, and it must be allowed that he appeared to appreciate to the full her tender care.

The diplomatic lawyer chose not to see the things which were patent. His greeting was,—

'I am glad to see you, Mr Holland, looking so much yourself. I was grieved to hear that you had had an accident.'

'Accident!' The reiteration was Miss Broad's. 'You call it accident!'

'My dear young lady, the words which lawyers use are not always intended to bear their strict dictionary significance.'

Another visitor was announced—Mr Horace Burton, as much at his ease as ever. Miss Broad blazed up at sight of him.

'You dare to come here!'

'Dare! Collyer, who's this young lady? Oh, it's Miss Broad, my future cousin. May I ask, Letty—you'll let me call you Letty?—why you should speak of my "daring" to come to my own lawyer's office? Hallo, Guy, you look squiffy! Buck up, my boy!'

He would have saluted his cousin with his open palm upon the back had not Miss Broad caught his arm as it was descending and flung it away. He gazed at her with what was meant for admiration.

'You are a warm one, Letty, really now! If you propose to slang Guy, as you seem fond of slanging me, you ought to have a pot of money to make it worth his while. He's likely to find marriage with you an expensive luxury, my dear.'

Mr Holland half rose from the chair on which Miss Broad had placed him. He spoke with hesitating tongue.

'You had better be careful—what you say.'

His relative laughed.

'You'd better be careful what you say, or you'll tumble down.'

Miss Broad laid her hand on Mr Holland's shoulder.

'Never mind what he says. I don't. He's not worth noticing.'

'Do you hear that, Collyer? Isn't she severe? But let's to business. I'm not come to engage in a tongue-match with a lady. The three months are up. Where's the ruby?'

Mr Collyer spoke.

'May I ask, Mr Holland, if you're in possession of the ring in question?'

It was Miss Broad who answered.

'No, he is not. Miss Bewicke calls herself his friend, and she even pretends to be mine, but her friendship does not go far enough to induce her to hand over property to its rightful owner which was never hers.'

Comment from Mr Burton,—

How sad! That's very wrong of her. Shows such deplorable moral blindness, doesn't it? She is a wicked woman, is May Bewicke—heartless, hypocritical, selfish to the core. Well, Collyer, anyhow that settles it. The money's mine, and I give you my personal assurance I can do with it.'

'I have not the slightest doubt of that, Mr Burton; but, before we conclude, there is something which I have been instructed to hand to Mr Holland. It was for that purpose I requested your presence here. Permit me, Mr Holland, to hand you this.'

From a drawer in his writing-table the lawyer produced a small parcel. When Mr Holland had undone, with somewhat shaky fingers, the outer covering, it was seen that within was a leather-covered case. Inside was a note, which he unfolded.

'Dear Guy,' it ran, 'this is a wedding present from yours, May Bewicke.'

'This' was a ring—the ring—the famous ruby.

While they gathered round it, with a babble of voices, and Mr Burton showed himself disposed to bluster, Miss Bewicke herself appeared at the door with Mr Bryan Dumville. She advanced to Mr Holland and Miss Broad.

'My dear children, how are you both? So you have the ring? That's all right. Directly I heard of the will, I sent it to Mr Collyer—he's my uncle, don't you know? I thought it would be safer with him than it would be with me. A lone, lorn woman's rooms are always open to the machinations of the most dreadful characters, and you never know what may happen—burglaries and all sorts of things. And you see I do call myself Guy's friend, and I even pretend, Letty, to be yours. Don't I, Bryan, dear?'

Some of the latter words suggested that the little lady had been listening outside the door. Mr Dumville confined his attention to Mr Horace Burton.

'So it's you again? I shall have to kill you after all.'

Actually Mr Burton did not seem altogether at his ease.

'I suppose, Guy, you couldn't let me have a thousand pounds to get away with?' He laughed. 'No; it's no good.

You'd better let me have it when I come out. They're waiting for me outside. A thousand would only be a drop in the sea. They wouldn't let me make a bolt of it for that.'

As he said, certain persons were waiting for him in the street. When he appeared, and it was discovered that he was not to have his uncle's money, within an hour he was arrested on a charge of forgery. It was a remarkable case, and not a savoury one. Neither prosecutors nor prisoner showed to advantage; but as it was clearly proved that Mr Horace Burton had forged, and put into circulation, a large number of acceptances and other legal documents, the jury had no option but to find him guilty. A hard-headed judge sent him to penal servitude for fourteen years.

The Flyman soon followed him, it was understood, to the same prison. His was a charge of robbery with violence in the City Road. The sand-bag again. As there were previous convictions against him, he suffered badly.

Mr Thomas Cox is still at large. He was seen lately on the cliff at Margate, with his wife and daughter, lounging on a chair listening to the band. He looked well and flourishing—an illustration of a sound mind in a sound body. But one never knows.

Mr Guy Holland and Mr Bryan Dumville were married at the same church, at the same time, on the same day. They are the best of friends. Their wives swear by one another. Mrs Guy Holland is convinced that Mrs Bryan Dumville is the most charming woman on the English stage, just as Mrs Bryan Dumville is certain that Mrs Guy Holland is the altogether most delightful person off it.

THE END